FRIGHT TIME

3 Spine-tingling Tales
for Young Readers

- NIGHT CREATURES
- WHO AM I?
- CEMETERY SCHOOL

BARONET
B·O·O·K·S

Baronet Books, New York, New York

FRIGHT TIME

edited by
Rochelle Larkin and Joshua Hanft

NIGHT CREATURES

by Shannon Donnelly

1

We call him Zooman."

I looked at the girl who had said that. She stood on the sidewalk not far from me, real close to the ambulance. I had seen her in front of the house across the street. And once at school. She had black hair and big dark eyes. I looked back at the ambulance and its flashing blue lights.

"No one knows his name so we call him Zooman," she said.

This time I frowned at her. I didn't want to make friends. I didn't want to like this town. It's only another boring town, I told myself. Just like the last three towns we had moved to. A boring town with boring people. I really wanted to believe that so that I wouldn't mind when we moved again.

"Don't you want to know why we call him that?" she said, starting to sound like I'd hurt her feelings. Shifting my backpack to my other hand, I looked at her again. She blinked and stared up at me.

I stuffed a hand in the back pocket of my jeans. "'Cause he works in the zoo, right?"

She shook her head and smiled. Then she pointed to the top of the wall.

I looked up at it, and didn't see anything but stones and a cloudy sky.

"Don't you see them? You can see the heads of some. Right near the top. Come on, you can see better from my house. They're called topiary," she said, pointing to the wall again.

"Topey-what?"

"Top-i-ary," she said slowly, like she was reading. "They're plants cut so that the leaves grow into animal shapes. See . . ." She pointed to a lump of green that looked like a picture of a dragon's head that I'd seen in a book. Its mouth

4

was open. "There's the ears on top and that's its nose and those bumps are its spine. Isn't it cool?"

"Yeah, I guess." I shrugged and started walking back across the street. She followed.

"He's got more. In his yard. Some are *really* cool. I saw them once when he first moved in and left his gate open. He moved here a long time before you did."

"Yeah, and I bet I move away before he does, too," I said. Not that I cared. Still, it was kind of different. I like animals. But it's hard to keep them when you move every year or two. "What kind of animals?" I asked.

"Not real animals. They're all make-believe. There's this really, really big bear with giant paws, and a lion with wings and . . ."

"Does he have any live animals? You know, like a cat?"

She shook her head. "Plants are alive. But I don't know about a cat. Do you have a cat?"

I shook my head. I'd had a cat, but I'd had to leave him behind when we moved.

Then I saw a blur of white.

"Watch out," I said and pulled the girl back.

The two ambulance guys came out through the gate as if the house behind them was on fire.

They had a stretcher with wheels. It looked like a long, flat shopping cart. One guy pulled, the other guy pushed. An old man lay on the stretcher, a blanket pulled up to his chin.

"Shut the gate, kid, will you?" the guy pulling the stretcher asked.

I nodded and grabbed the black iron handle. I had to push with both hands to clang it shut. Then I turned around.

As I did, I heard the old man talking. "Can't leave . . . won't let me . . . they won't . . . have to feed . . . animals . . . feed . . ."

I looked up to ask the guys if they had seen any cats or dogs in the yard, but they were busy.

Blue lights flashed. The siren started screaming again and the ambulance drove away.

When it had gone, the girl looked up at me. "Do you really think he was talking about his plant animals?"

I shrugged, then I walked back over to the gate.

The gate must have locked when I shut it. I pulled at the handle, but it didn't move. "Hold this," I said, giving the girl my backpack. I found a part of the wall where the rocks stuck out a lot. "Warn me if you see the bus," I said. Then I quickly started to climb. It was tough.

By the time I hooked my elbows over the wall top, I was panting like I'd run all the way to school. I pulled my weight up and then balanced on my elbows. The stone scraped, but I didn't care because now I could see everything in the old man's yard.

I stopped counting the number of plant-animals when I reached twelve. They filled his yard. Mystical animals. Giant animals. I saw the bear the girl had told me about. It had to be twice as big as a real bear and had bare branches that stuck out of giant paws like wood knives. A big dark bush had the shape of a tiger with two giant, curved fangs. I couldn't see the lion with wings, but I saw all of the dragon. It grew from a yellow-green plant that had four roots, one for each foot. It had short wings and teeth and the yellow-green leaves made it look like it had scales. When the wind made the leaves move, the dragon looked like it was breathing.

I balanced on my elbows, my mouth dry from hanging open. I couldn't stop staring.

The wind blew the hair into my eyes. It made the leaves of the plants move and brush each other so that they sounded like people whispering. It sounded like the plants were talking. The hair on the back of my arm stood up. I got this creepy feeling like something in the yard had suddenly looked up and seen me.

2

"Hey! The bus is coming!"

Glancing down, I lost my balance and fell backward. I grabbed at the wall and my fingers caught on the top. My toe found a rock and I hung there for a second. Then I got my other foot on a rock and was able to start climbing down.

"Hurry!" the girl shouted, hopping up and down.

"Go ahead," I yelled down.

She ran for the bus, taking my backpack with her. I watched the bus drive off with her *and* my backpack.

I skinned my fingers, scraped my knuckles and tore my jeans getting down the wall. Then I had a long walk to school.

I spent most of the day wondering if the old man had some kind of animal other than his plants. I wanted to get a better look. I felt sure that I had seen something and something had seen me. I knew it.

It took forever until the school bell rang and I got home.

"Warren, is that you?" Mom yelled as I slammed the door behind me. "Can you take the trash out and then run to the store for me?"

Mom kept me busy until almost dinnertime. Then I put my Swiss Army knife, the one Dad gave me last year, into my jacket pocket. I hid a can of tuna in my other pocket and went out the back door, yelling that I was going out to play.

The sun had gone down and the streetlights were just flickering on. The sky had turned purple at the top and yellow on the sides. I would have just enough light to climb over the wall and unlock the gate from the inside.

I stared up at the wall for a while, telling myself that I could do it. Then I started to climb.

It seemed easier than it had in the morning. I got to the top and pulled myself up so that I could sit there. I heard the leaves "shushing" against each other, like they were telling someone to be quiet.

Then I looked down into the yard.

It looked black. Like the ground wasn't there

anymore. Like a black pit. I could see the tops of the animal plants sticking up out of that pit. The streetlight behind me gave the plants weird shadows and made the leaves not look like leaves anymore. Instead, the plants looked as if they were solid bodies. I shuddered and pulled my jacket closer. They were just plants, I told myself. Just plants.

My plan had been to climb down one of the topiary trees. If I stretched my legs out, I knew I would be standing on the dragon's nose. Now, I didn't like the idea of my foot next to the pointy branches I had seen that morning. I told myself that it was just that I didn't want to get poked by the branches. But I really didn't want my foot anywhere near that dragon's wooden teeth.

So I twisted around and started climbing down the rocks.

Going down seemed harder. My foot slipped. I scrambled to get my shoe onto another rock.

Then I got that feeling again.

Something had seen me. Something was watching.

I turned, fingernails digging into rock edges. I stared at the ground until my eyes ached, but I didn't see anything but green shadows. The wind whipped my hair into my eyes, making them sting. My arms ached from hanging there. I had to get down. The wind gusted. Branches rattled. Then one swiped at my back. Another hit my hands, stabbing me like claws. I yelled, but the wall and the wind muffled the sound.

I tried to hang on, but I couldn't. My fingers slipped. I grabbed for a better hold on another rock, but I missed. My hand closed over smooth rock, then slid away.

I started falling.

3

I hit the ground with a thud that knocked the air out of me. I felt like someone had stepped on my chest. Dad would kill me if I'd broken anything, like a rib or bone. I got down a mouthful of air and was able to sit.

The sky seemed darker from inside the wall. I couldn't see anything but the plants around me.

I got up, trying to be real quiet. I didn't know why I should be quiet, I just felt that I should.

From the ground, I couldn't even see the old

man's house, there were so many plants. The plants looked a lot bigger from down here, too.

"Here, kitty," I said, keeping my voice low. I tried not to be such a sissy and said louder, "Here, kitty."

The bushes around me rustled in the wind. I decided to stop calling and just look around.

The old man had planted his animals—his topiary—so that each had its own space in the yard. I walked right between them, keeping as far away from them as I could. They were a lot creepier up close. I shivered. I felt like a caterpillar was walking along the back of my neck. I felt like someone was watching me.

Then I looked up and saw it.

It sat right in front of the house. Three times as big as me. It had a mouth wide enough that I could fit my head into it if I wanted to. I couldn't see what kind of plant it was, but I could see the shape the old man had given it. It looked like a lion. A big lion. A big lion with wings.

I couldn't stop staring.

It had one paw up, like it was going to swipe at me. The old man—the Zooman—had cut the wood so that the lion looked like it had claws. Real claws that poked out from leafy paws. The wood claws gleamed in the streetlight, looking white and sharp.

"It's just a plant," I muttered. I stuffed my hands into my pockets. My fingers closed around my Swiss Army knife. It felt good to hold it.

Keeping one hand around my knife, I pulled out my other hand. I would prove that it was just a plant.

I reached up, watching the plant as I did so. It didn't move. Slowly, I touched a leaf, then jerked my hand back as if I had tapped a stove to feel if it was hot. Nothing happened. I reached out again, feeling better about it now. It was kind of fun to be in here on my own. If I reached up high, I could touch its face.

"Ow!" I pulled back my hand. Something sharp had dug into my finger. Putting my finger in my mouth, I tasted blood. It must have thorns, I thought, edging away.

I kept my eye on the winged lion-plant as I looked around the yard. I didn't like it. I didn't like any of it. Mostly, I really didn't like that lion-plant.

Around the side, I found a metal shed.

The shed door was open, but the inside was too dark to see anything. I wished that I had brought Dad's big flashlight, or my own pocket light. Pushing open the shed door, I could see a little better, but all I saw was a sack. I pulled it out and held it up to see.

Bonemeal.

That's what the label read in big, dark letters. It had a musty, dry smell just like what I thought old bones would smell like. I closed the sack and put it back in the shed.

Then I heard something rustle behind me.

I whirled around. It wasn't the wind this time. I would have felt the wind. Something else had made the plant leaves move. I dug my hand into my pocket again. I stared into the yard, but I didn't see anything move.

I knelt down and pulled out my knife and the can of tuna. I opened the can and left it next to one of the plant-animals near the shed. The old man had probably left the shed open for his cat. That's what I thought.

Then I walked to the gate.

I kept looking over my shoulder as I walked. The wind had started to blow again. It made the leaves move so that they sounded like people talking in really low, quiet voices. I twisted around so that I could see the lion-plant with wings. I wanted to make sure that it still sat by the house. That it hadn't stretched out its wings and pulled its roots out of the ground.

Instead, I felt leaves and branches brush my arm.

I yelled and jumped back. Tripping over my own feet, I fell. I stared up at the giant bear. Its arm blocked the path to the gate. I had run straight into it.

Heart pounding, I got to my feet. I ran to the gate. I didn't look back once. I didn't want to see if the bear had turned around to watch me.

I ran so fast that I slammed into the wooden gate. My hand closed over the metal latch. It took two tries for me to get my fingers around that latch. Then I pushed the gate open. I almost fell onto the sidewalk.

Outside, standing under the streetlight, I turned around.

I felt like a dope. With the streetlight streaming through the gateway, the plants all looked like plants. The bear hadn't turned around. I had just run into it and scared myself. I peered into the gloom, looking for the lion with the wings. It sat there beside the house, both paws folded in front of it. Its wings looked like vines now and nothing like wings. Funny, but I had thought one paw had been up.

"Warrrr-ennnn!" Mom sounded like she wanted me home now. I made sure the gate wouldn't lock behind me, then I slammed it closed and ran for my house.

"Hi. Do you want this back?

I looked up from my lunch. The dark-haired girl from across the street held out my backpack.

"Yeah. Thanks." I took the backpack and put it on the ground beside me. I looked at my sandwich, then at the girl. "You like baloney?"

She wrinkled her nose and shook her head. Then she sat down on the bench opposite me. "I'll trade you half my peanut-butter for your apple."

We made the swap, sandwich for apple. Between crunches, she said, "My name's Carrie."

"I'm Warren," I said.

"I know." She pointed to my backpack. "It's on your bag. Did you find any cats in the Zooman's yard?"

I sat there, sandwich halfway to my mouth, staring at her.

"I saw you climb into his yard. I can see a lot from my room. It's at the top of the stairs."

16

I asked if she knew where the hospital was.
"Why?"
"Because I have to see him."
"Who? The Zooman?"
"Yeah. I want to ask about his animals." I had stopped by the old man's yard again this morning. It didn't look too spooky in daylight. And it wasn't hard getting in and out with the gate unlocked. Even so, I didn't stay long. Just long enough to find out that the tuna can wasn't there. Something had eaten the tuna. And had taken the can away, too. The old man probably had several cats and one of them dragged the tuna away to eat it. That's what I told Carrie. I wasn't really so sure *what* had eaten the tuna. That's why I wanted to see the Zooman.

"I can show you how to get there after school," she said. "If we get off the bus at the end of town, we can walk to it."

I thought about this. It was my idea to talk to the Zooman. But I decided that it was okay if she came along. It still didn't mean that we were friends or anything.

It took longer than I thought it would to walk to the hospital. We had to walk to almost where the street turned and went out into the country.

Behind the hospital, pine trees marked the start of the forest.

I made Carrie wait in the front where they had some chairs and magazines. I gave her my backpack to hold while she waited. A lady dressed in pink and white looked up as I stopped at her wooden desk. That's when I realized that I was in trouble.

"Can I help you?" she asked.

What could I say, I want to see the Zooman? I didn't even know the old man's name. I stuffed my hands in my back pockets. "Uhm...some guys brought in an old man yesterday, and, uh...well, I live next door."

She looked at me the way my mom does when I've asked her if I can do something and she's about to tell me no in a really nice way. "Do you know his name?" she asked.

I looked at Carrie, who had her nose pressed up against the window and was turning her head to see a brown sparrow perched on the bush outside.

I looked back at the nurse. "Uh, I'm supposed to take care of his animals, but I need to ask him something."

"Why don't you come back with your parents.

18

Visiting hours are until eight." She picked up a clipboard and walked away.

I stood there for a minute. Then I followed her.

The place hadn't looked that big from the outside. It was that big. I walked until I got lost. Then I started following old-people sounds.

I could hear old people talking to themselves, muttering just like the old man had. I kept poking down halls, listening. I avoided the sounds of people walking, shoes sharp on the floor. I stayed away from the crying babies. I walked like I knew where I was going.

I was about to turn around and head back when I heard a woman say, "Vera, I can't get these forms done! All he can talk about is taking care of his animals. I don't even know what he keeps that would worry him so much."

Hiding in a doorway, I watched as the woman talking and another one walked past me. They both had on white pants and tops. When they turned the corner, I came out and started looking into every room. One of them had to be the one that the nurses had come out of. One of them had to be the Zooman's room.

I opened another door and poked my head inside. Then I heard him. "Feed . . . must . . . won't let me go . . . can't take them . . ."

The windows had curtains over them so that it looked like night. A light was on in one corner. It gave off a yellow glow that made everything in the room look sick. The muttering came from the bed. The only other things in the room were a chair and a tray thing that could be moved. I stepped into the room, edging toward him.

The old man looked really small and thin. He had tubes stuck in his arms and he lay there with his eyes closed. His hair looked like cotton balls that had been pulled apart and stuck to the sides of his head with glue.

"Take care . . . must take them . . ." he muttered, sounding like he was talking in his sleep.

"Mister," I said, leaning over him. It smelled bad. Like a stale bathroom and the stuff Mom uses to clean the floors. "Mister?" I said again.

He turned his head away from me.

I touched his arm. His skin felt dry and cool. The place where I touched stayed dented, like it was a soft pillow. "Mister, what kind of animals do you have?"

"Trim . . . have to . . ."

What kind of cats needed trimming? Maybe he had mixed up trimming his plants and feeding his cats. "Do you have a dog?" I asked, though I knew that I would have heard a dog barking if he had one.

"Get them . . . meal . . . go . . . "

He was falling asleep. His breathing got deep and steady. I shook him lightly again, but he didn't say anything. So I left his room and shut the door behind me.

"Is he going to come home?" Carrie asked as we turned the corner onto our street.

I shrugged and shifted my backpack to my other shoulder. "Maybe. But not for a while." I looked down the street to his house. I could see the tops of the plant animals. They almost looked like they were trying to see over the top of the wall.

"Are you sure he said that he wanted you to feed his cats?" Carrie asked. She'd asked me that same question five times now.

I frowned at her. "I told you, he didn't say much. But he's got something that needs feeding. And that's what I'm going to do."

I put out more tuna that night. I made sure to get over to the Zooman's house right after school and before it got dark. Then I went home to count my allowance money. At this rate, Mom was going to notice the missing tuna. I'd go to the store tomorrow and buy some real cat food. Maybe a bag of it.

The plants started to look real bad the next week. Branches had grown out of the bear's head, making it look like it had bull-horns. All the animals looked a little shaggy. The lion's mane had gotten bigger. Lots bigger. So had its wings. And the dragon no longer looked like it had bumps on its back. Now it looked like a cat that had arched way up to make itself bigger. All their claws and teeth still looked sharp.

I had put out a bag of cat food every night for the past week. Every morning I checked and the bag would be gone. Not just the food, but the whole bag. I couldn't figure out what would eat the bag. There was only one way for me to find out. I would have to go there at night and see what happened.

That night, I waited until I heard Mom and Dad shut off the TV. When the door to their bedroom clicked shut, I counted to one hundred. Then I got out of bed and pulled on my jeans, my sneakers and a sweatshirt. I grabbed my backpack and sneaked out the back door. I already had packed everything I would need in the backpack—Dad's flashlight, more cat food and my Swiss Army knife.

The streetlight seemed really bright as I stepped out onto the sidewalk. I walked toward the gate, thinking that maybe this wasn't such a good idea. Only two things kept me from turning around and going back to my room. One was that I hadn't put out any food that night for the Zooman's animals. The other was that Carrie might be watching and I didn't want to look like a chicken. I glanced at Carrie's house. There were lights on downstairs. I saw the bluish flicker of a TV in the living room. The room upstairs—the one that had to be Carrie's—looked dark.

I turned at the wall and stopped in front of the gate. Then I took a very deep breath and went inside.

The yard looked really spooky. The plants had grown even more. The bear looked like it had new claws growing out of its paws. The dragon looked more like a dinosaur—the kind with armor stuff around its neck and horns on its head. The lion still looked like a lion, but the wings now looked like they had feathers sprouting.

I tried not to look at the topiaries as I crept around to the shed.

The shed's metal door creaked as I opened it. I clicked on Dad's flashlight. The light hit the wall, bouncing around like a glowing ball. I left the bag of cat food out near the plants and then came back to sit in the shed. I would watch for an hour and then go home. I glanced at my watch. It was only a little past ten o'clock.

I sat there until I felt cold all the way through. I tried to keep my hands warm by holding them under my armpits, but that meant that I had to shut off my flashlight. That was okay until the moon rose.

The plants looked worse in the moonlight.

In the dark, I couldn't see anything but outlines. But when the moon came up, the silver light pulled weird shadows and shapes out of the plants. Against the sky, they looked bigger than ever. The wind came up and I heard branches creaking. Leaves rustled and the creepy feeling came back that something was watching me.

I tucked my feet together, resting my chin on my knees and thought about leaving. Only, to get out, I had to walk by the plants again. Maybe I should wait just a little longer. I could wait until the wind stopped.

Then I heard the gate creak open.

4

I held my breath and sat real still. I could hear my heart pounding. Was someone coming in, or was something going out? I had been good at hide-and-seek when I was a kid. Now I tried to remember how to play. Only I wasn't playing. I really was hiding.

The wind creaked through the plants again. The plant-animals bowed their heads as if they were looking down at something. Maybe looking for something small, like me. In the wind, the bear's paw looked like it was waving. Then a light flashed on and I heard laughing.

"Come on, over here!"

The light bobbed around like a blind ghost. I watched it, squinting to try and see better.

"Get the shovels. Ouch! Not on my foot!"

Another light switched on and in its glow I saw three older boys. I knew them from school. They were two grades up from me and a lot bigger. I stayed in the shed and out of the reach of their flashlights.

"All right, you said you'd trash the place. Let's see!" the biggest kid said. He held his flashlight higher. They started to laugh.

The other two had shovels. One of them stepped out of the light. I heard digging. The other boy looked around at the plants. "Hey, Jerry, I don't know if . . ."

The kid talking got a whack on his shoulder from Jerry, the biggest kid. "You wimping out, wimp?"

Rubbing his shoulder, the kid shook his head no. He looked sick, but he moved. Jerry laughed. He set his flashlight on the ground and then moved into the darkness. Now I couldn't see them, but I could hear them digging. What were they doing? Burying something? Digging something up?

My stomach turned over. What if they were digging up the plants?

It took me a while to work up the nerve to leave the shed. I didn't want to, but the idea that they might be digging up the plants made my stomach ache. I don't know why it bothered me so much. But it did. I liked the idea that the plants had roots that held them in the ground. I felt bad for the old man. How would he feel if he came home and found his yard trashed? Would it make him need to go back to the hospital?

I crept forward. I didn't want to get too close to the plant animals, but I didn't want to step into the beam left by Jerry's flashlight.

Then I heard a worse sound.

Chopping.

I froze. I could hear the thunk of an ax as it bit into wood. Thunk. Thunk. Thunk. The wind picked up, making the plants around me shiver. I shivered, too. Swallowing hard, I stood up. Someone had to stop them. I was the only someone around.

I stepped forward and turned on my own flashlight. The light darted around, showing the bear's horned-head, the tiger's overgrown tail, the dragon's arched back.

The sound of the ax was still going. I heard the kids laughing. The laughter went from tree to tree, from topiary to topiary, from shadowy creature to shadowy creature. The boys seemed to be everywhere, cutting, digging. I hated it. I hated them suddenly.

"Hey!" I yelled, almost scaring myself. "Hey! Stop it!"

A face came out of the darkness. I swung the light onto it. I had to look up to see Jerry's face. He was a big kid with orange hair and yellow eyes. His eyes looked a lot like the eyes I had seen on that lion in the zoo. They didn't have any fear in them.

The other two boys came up behind Jerry. They looked at each other. Dirt stuck to the blades of their shovels. Jerry held the ax.

"What do you want?" he demanded.

I wanted to yell at him to stop doing what he was doing and go home. But I couldn't get those words out. I just wet my lips and said, "This isn't your yard." I wished that I sounded like my dad when he got mad.

"And it's yours, shrimp?" Jerry said. He pushed my shoulder, making me stumble back. My foot knocked his flashlight, making it roll in the grass. The light spun weird shadows off the plants around us. "Well, is it?"

"You aren't supposed to be here," I said, trying something else. "If you don't stop, I'll tell the old man who lives here what you did."

Jerry laughed. "Oh, I'm scared. Real scared. You scared, guys?" He looked at the other two boys. They looked over their shoulders like they had heard something. They looked scared.

"I'm telling you . . ." I started.

Jerry turned and socked me. His fist slammed

into my shoulder, knocking me down. I got up, my face hot. Stepping forward, I swung at him. As I did, I heard the wind yowl behind me. It whipped the leaves. Leaves shook as I grunted and swung. Branches snapped as my fist swooshed, hitting only air.

Jerry screamed and fell back.

I couldn't see much. My flashlight was pointing down and Jerry's was pointed at the bushes. I stood over Jerry. I kept the hand that didn't have the flashlight in a fist.

Jerry rolled over. He was crying. He had three long gashes on his face. I looked down at my fist. I knew I hadn't made those gashes. I went cold all over. The leaves kept rustling, but I realized that I couldn't feel my hair move. I lifted my face. Not a breath of wind brushed against it.

The leaves kept rustling.

Slowly, I started to turn toward the rustling. It was like I had to look, like I couldn't do anything else but look. My heart pounded like I had been running. I turned, twisting at the waist, feet rooted to the ground. I was in one of those dreams where you want to move fast, only the more you try to hurry, the less you can move.

Jerry's flashlight still lay on its side. In its

light I saw the bushes that the other boys had pulled out of the ground. My heart started hammering. I saw two empty holes where the bear-plant had stood. It should have been lying on the ground. It wasn't.

I looked up.

The bear-plant stood there, taller than it had been when it was rooted in the ground. Dirt dripped off twisted, bare roots like blood clots off bony fingers. It swayed as if a strong wind was blowing. Only there wasn't any wind. Wood creaked and leaves shivered as it moved. Slowly, it lifted its head. Dark holes showed where the eyes should have been. It pushed its nose forward, making a snuffling sound.

I opened my mouth.

Nothing came out. I didn't have enough spit to scream. My eyes felt like they were going to pop out of my head. I watched as the bear-thing shuffled one twisted root forward. Its giant paw-shaped branch rose like it was being pulled up with a rope. Only there wasn't any rope. It moved on its own. Its claws shone white in the moonlight.

Then the paw-branch started to fall toward me.

5

I fell backward over Jerry. The paw-branch swung down, leaves catching on my jacket and tearing it. Behind me, the other boys screamed. I heard a clatter as the boys dropped their shovels. I heard sneakers thudding on the dirt. Then I scrambled to my feet. I pulled at Jerry's jacket and yelled at him.

"See what you did! See!"

Jerry wasn't looking. He got to his feet and ran for the gate. I heard something behind me and turned.

They had cut the winged lion off its roots. Its head turned, twisting on its thick branches. Then it rolled to its feet, the way a tumbleweed rolls. One wing flapped, making its own wind, and then the other. It threw back its head, only instead of a roar it sounded like someone holding a branch and shaking it real hard. I felt sick. Then I started running.

The other boys had shut the gate behind them when they came in. Now, they crowded around it, pushing at each other. Jerry pulled the others away and grabbed at the gate handle. He was crying, sobbing like a little kid. I could see the three gashes in his face. They looked like black lines. He jerked real hard on the handle and it came loose in his hand.

"The wall! Climb!" I yelled. I glanced back. I could see the topiary moving, shifting, shuffling. The air smelled like wet dirt. I heard leaves crackling, branches creaking. The plant-things moved slowly, but they were so big! They made that snuffling sound, like a big dog smelling a rabbit's trail.

I turned quickly and started to climb. The other boys were over the top before I was half-way. I heard their sneakers hit the sidewalk. I heard them swearing and running. The sound of their sneakers slamming against the pavement disappeared into the night, leaving me panting and trying to climb.

Rocks scraped my fingers. I heard the plants moving again and something worse—I heard the beating of wings.

How long would it take the lion-thing to learn how to fly? Would it find me on the wall and just grab me? Could it wrap its branches around my arms and fly away with me?

I climbed faster.

Behind me, I heard something tear. I remembered the cat food. They had found it. They were tearing the bag open. Maybe I did have time.

Then I felt something grab my ankle.

I kicked at it, but it came back, grabbing at me again. It wrapped around my ankle so tight that I thought my shoe and sock would come off. My leg stung. I kicked again and it let go. Then I hauled myself over the wall. I didn't even think about the drop down to the ground as I swung over and let myself dangle. Then I let go.

I fell on my feet and crumpled up like I didn't have any bones. Suddenly, hands grabbed my arm and pulled me up.

6

"Get up! Hurry! Come on!" Carried dragged at my arm. We staggered to her front door. She slammed it shut behind us. I sank down on her floor.

She squatted down beside me, her eyes really big. "I saw. I saw them move," she whispered. It was real quiet in her house. It smelled like warm cookies and dinner.

I turned to her. "They dug them up," I said, between gasps for air. "They dug them up and cut them down."

She looked at the door. "They're real, aren't they? The Zooman's animals?"

I nodded. I got up but I didn't want to look out her windows. I wanted to stay behind her locked door. I didn't know if the plant-things could get through doors, but I wanted to hope. "They're real. And they aren't held down by roots anymore."

I stayed at her house. She pulled out a sleeping bag and I curled up in her big brother's old room. I didn't sleep, so I didn't have any trouble leaving when the sun came up. I ran across the street to my own house, not even looking at the gray wall around the Zooman's house. I didn't want to see the plant tops moving. Maybe the wall would keep them in.

Then I remembered the lion with the wings.

Mom asked if I was feeling all right when she saw me at breakfast. She said I looked pale. I said I was fine. I kept my scraped hands out of sight. She didn't notice my missing backpack and I didn't talk about it. I didn't mind going to school. I didn't mind going anywhere that was away from the Zooman's house.

I didn't see Carrie at school. But I saw the two other boys and Jerry. They looked at me once, then acted like they had never seen me before. I heard from another guy that Jerry got called into the principal's office and asked if he got cut in a fight. I didn't hear what he had answered, but I could guess that he wasn't going to tell the truth about it.

I spent the day trying to figure out what I was going to say about last night. Or even who I should tell. I walked home instead of taking the bus.

Carrie was sitting outside her house.

"Nothing's happened. Do you think they left?" she asked, skipping over to me. She kept looking at the Zooman's house. So did I. I couldn't see anything over the wall. Not even the tops of the plants.

I shrugged. "I don't know."

"What're you going to do?" she asked.

I stared at the wall. "Wait and see, I guess." That's what my dad said when he wasn't sure. Maybe it would work for me, too.

I waited four days. Carrie kept telling me about the stuff she heard her parents talking about. I heard it from mine, too. A poodle was missing from a house down the street. Then a cat.

Dad talked about coyotes coming down from the forest. Only coyotes don't slash car tires, I thought to myself. Carrie's mom had found her car with the tires all cut up the morning after the boys had been in the Zooman's yard. Coyotes also don't leave inch-long scratches on doors. Those showed up on our front door. And coyotes don't rip open metal garbage cans and eat everything inside. That happened all over the street on trash night.

The next morning I was sitting on the curb with Carrie. "It's getting worse, isn't it?" she said. "Mom doesn't want me out after dark. She thinks it's gang kids."

I scraped my knife blade along the curb. "I think I know what to do."

"What?"

I looked at her. "Replant them. And feed them that bonemeal stuff. I think I can buy another sack of it at the hardware store."

She wrinkled her nose. "Do you think it's made from real bones?" She shivered as if it was cold, even though the sun was out.

I shrugged. "I've got to do something soon. I don't like that people's cats are missing."

"They could have been scared away."

I nodded. That's what I hoped, too. I stood and folded up my knife. "I'm putting them in today. After school." I waited, sort of hoping that she might offer to help. She didn't. I didn't blame her. I didn't want to do it, either. But I felt it was my fault for unlocking the gate in the first place. And I didn't feel right about asking her to help. We weren't even friends. So I turned and walked back to my house.

Mom had errands for me when I got home from school. Then I had to finish my homework. The sun had turned into an orange ball above Carrie's house when Mom finally let me get out of the house. I tried not to think about the time. Grabbing Dad's shovel, I headed for the best climbing spot in the wall.

I had figured out a quick way in and out since the gate was still broken. I wished that I could wait until Saturday to do this. But I didn't want any more cats disappearing. Plus, I wasn't sure that if I waited, the plant-things wouldn't get hungry for something bigger.

The bonemeal sack was too heavy to carry. I

tied a rope around it so that I could pull it up to the top of the wall. I just threw the shovel over the wall. I didn't care what it landed on. Then I started climbing.

I had bought a pair of work gloves at the hardware store. They made climbing easier. Once I got to the top of the wall, I pulled the sack up and used the rope to lower it to the ground on the other side.

The yard looked like tractors had dug it up. Big holes dotted the ground. Around the holes, the grass had died. The plants all lay on their sides. They still had glossy green leaves. I noticed that the lion-plant had started to grow new roots from the stumps where it had been cut down.

I didn't have much time, so I just dug down in the holes that were already there. I wanted the bear-thing in the ground first. After I dug the hole, I had to grab it. I hoped that it would stay asleep or whatever it was.

The branch twisted in my hold. It moved, wiggling like a real thick, slow worm. I let go and jumped back, but it didn't get up. I pulled my gloves on tighter and grabbed it again.

I hated touching it. It didn't stay still like

wood. It didn't feel like wood. It didn't feel like anything I'd ever touched before. Up close, the leaves had a funny smell, like inside a closet. The branches tore at my jacket and jeans as I struggled. I got the bear-thing into the hole and started shoveling dirt back in. Then I got busy with the others.

I kept looking up at the sky as I worked. It got dark fast in the Zooman's yard. The dark crept up from under the wall. I wanted the sunlight to wait for me. I didn't want to get caught there again. But I couldn't work any faster. I was already sweating. My arms ached. I could feel blisters swelling under my gloves.

It was almost dark by the time I got the last one replanted. I did the lion-plant last. I kept thinking that I saw it move as I worked. I stopped work, held my breath and stared at it. When it kept still, I started working even faster. Since Jerry had cut the lion-plant's legs, I had to dig a new hole for it.

By then, the wind had started again. Every time it stirred the leaves, I jumped. I swatted as the wind blew leaves into my face. The wind tossed the branches, which grabbed at me like bony fingers. Every time they did, my heart thudded up to my throat. Almost done, I kept telling myself.

Straightening, my back popped. I pulled off my gloves and looked up. The sky was turning soft purple. Around me, leaves shivered in the breeze. The wind felt cold on my face. Then the wind stopped.

I froze. I listened. Had I heard something rustle? Something move? Something stir without the wind to make it stir? I swallowed, but my mouth felt dry. I glanced at the wall. Could I make it in time?

Then I felt the fingers clamp down on my shoulder.

7

With a yell, I swung around. I fell over the bonemeal sack and landed on the grass.

Carrie squeaked and jumped back.

I sat up and glared at her. "What are you doing here?"

She looked around, eyes big and scared. "I came to help. You were taking so long. It's almost dark."

Getting up, I picked up the bag of bonemeal. "Yeah, I know. All that's left to do now is spread this around."

She wrinkled her nose, but she put her hands together as I told her to. I tore open the bag and poured some of the powder into her hands. She wasn't to get too close to the plants, but to throw the white dust at them from three feet away.

"How deep did you plant them?" she asked, hands out for more bonemeal. "Mom tells Daddy that she wants her bulbs planted two feet deep."

I frowned. "I think I got them deeper than that."

The wind picked up, making the plants shiver.

"What's that?" Carrie spun around.

"Just the wind. Come on, we've got to do the lion."

Carrie was shaking by the time we got to the lion. So was I, only I kept it inside. We had used up most of the bonemeal. A lot of it ended up on my jeans and Carrie's sweatshirt. The stuff stuck to everything just like chalk dust.

I threw a couple of handfuls at the lion. It leaned in its new hole like a crooked Christmas tree, only I'd never seen a tree look mean before. I got the feeling that it didn't like what I had done. I started to worry.

"Can we go now?" Carrie whispered.

I nodded. The creepy feeling was back. The feeling that something was watching.

We ran over to where I had left the rope. I threw Dad's shovel over and told Carrie, "Climb up, then slide down the rope. I'll hold it for you."

She nodded and started climbing.

She wasn't a good climber. I had to boost her to get her started. It took her a long time to reach the top. By the time she got there, it was a lot darker. Sweat trickled down my shoulder blades, but I felt too hot for my jacket. I braced my weight against the rope and told Carrie to slide down. The rope went loose when she reached the ground on the other side.

Then I heard the leaves rustling again.

I looked over my shoulder. It was dark now. Stars glistened overhead. I heard that snuffling again and a weird sucking sound. I looked down at the bag of bonemeal.

"Hold the rope with all your weight," I called to Carrie as loud as I dared. Behind me, the sounds stopped.

The hair on my neck stood up. I started climbing, using the rope so that I could go faster. At the top, I had to stop. I had to see if they were going to stay in the ground.

"Warren?" Carried called, her voice quiet.

I shushed her and listened. The sucking sound got louder. It seemed to come from everywhere. The streetlight flickered on and I got a better look.

The plant-things rocked right and left like someone had a teeter-totter under them. I stared at the inky ground. I hadn't put them in deep enough. The sucking sound came from their trying to pull their roots up. Then it stopped.

"What's happening?" Carrie whispered.

I started climbing down the wall. When I reached the ground, I slumped down, feeling tired. "I think it worked."

She looked up and smiled. Then her smile went away. Her mouth formed an O. I looked up, too.

The tiger-plant crouched on top of the wall. Fresh dirt clung to the root-paws that I had put into the ground. I hadn't planted it deep enough! It had pulled free again. It swung its head around, wood creaking. Its long fangs had grown so much that they scraped on the wall.

Grabbing Carrie's hand, I pulled her against

the wall. Then I started crawling along, one hand dragging Carrie.

I heard it snuffling. Carrie didn't make a sound. I glanced at her. She hadn't stopped staring at the tiger-creature. I grabbed her face and made her look away from it.

"We have to get to my house," I whispered.

I heard leaves rustle on top of the wall. Then the rustling fell to the ground. It had jumped into my yard.

Hanging onto Carrie, I got to my feet and started running. I zigzagged like when I used to play spies in one of my old neighborhoods. Behind me, I heard the tiger-thing still snuffling. It was tracking us.

I tripped on something and fell. "Keep going," I shouted to Carrie. Getting up, I grabbed what had tripped me. It was Dad's shovel. I grabbed it with both hands like it was a baseball bat. I grabbed the handle end and turned. I could hear the tiger-thing rustling as it moved. I waited as long as I could. Then I swung.

The shovel connected with the tiger's head. I saw one wood saber-tooth snap. I heard branches break. I heard more rustling as the thing fell back. I threw the shovel at it, then turned and ran for the back door.

Carrie held the door open slightly. "Hurry!" she shouted.

I ran inside and slammed the door behind me. I still heard the thing outside. Branches scratched against the door. It sounded like a hurricane wanting to get in.

Mom came into the kitchen and gave me a funny look. Then she saw Carrie and smiled. "Well, what have you two been up to? Warren, you'd better get that jacket off and into the laundry right now. My word, the wind sure is kicking up tonight. It's almost howling through those trees. Would your friend like to stay to dinner?"

Carrie and I just looked at each other.

"He's down here," I told Carrie. We had snuck into the hospital after school the next day. I looked down the empty hallway, and then Carrie and I headed for the Zooman's room.

"Do you think he'll know how to get rid of them?" Carrie asked, staring up at the pictures on the pale green walls.

"They're his plants."

"Then why didn't *he* get rid of them?" She frowned at me and pulled off her jacket.

"Maybe he didn't want to. Or maybe he was too sick to. You heard what the guys who brought him here said. He probably hasn't been able to do much for a long time. Now, be quiet." I poked my head into the Zooman's room. Motioning Carrie to follow me, I stepped inside.

The curtains were open and I could see the mountains and pine trees. I walked over to the old man.

"Uh oh, it looks like someone hit him," Carrie said.

I wasn't feeling too good. The old man had a purple bruise across the lower part of his face, like someone had hit him with a shovel. I tugged the blanket off his feet. He had cuts around his legs. Cuts like those that the lion-plant had around *its* legs.

"Carrie, look," I said, pointing. I told her about my hitting the tiger-plant with the shovel. I put the blanket down again. "What if we set the plants on fire and the Zooman burns as well? He's got cuts, just like the lion-thing. And he's got a bruise just where I hit that tiger!"

We stood there staring at the Zooman. I kept wishing he would wake up and tell us something.

"What are you kids doing in here!"

The voice made both of us jump. We whirled around. The nurse I had seen the other day stood glaring at us.

"Uh, we . . . " I stammered.

Stepping forward, Carrie said, "We live next door to him. Is he going to get better?"

The nurse stopped looking so mad. She bent down so that her face was at the same level as Carrie's. "I'm sorry. He got worse last night. Much worse."

Carrie looked at me.

"Come on," I said, tugging at Carrie's jacket. At the door, I thought of something and turned around. "Uh, has he said anything . . . I mean, about his . . . his animals?"

The nurse shook her head, then looked at the Zooman. "Nothing about animals. But, well, he wanted someone to do something for him. Poor man. He couldn't get past asking, would I go— only he couldn't say where."

Outside the hospital, I zipped up my jacket. It had turned cold.

"What now?" Carrie asked.

I stuffed my hands into my pockets and started walking down the street. Then I stopped and turned to stare at the hospital. The trees rose up tall behind the building. "Would...would... what had the old man wanted the nurse to do? 'Would you go?' Go *where*?"

I looked at the trees again. Then I grabbed Carrie's arm and turned her to face me. "I know. I know what he wanted! But how do we....I know! Just like the coyotes. He couldn't do it, but maybe *we* can!"

"Do what?" Carrie asked, sounding like she thought I was crazy.

Letting go of her arm, I wondered if I should ask. I couldn't do it alone. I needed help. "Coyotes hunt in pairs," I said, talking fast. "If one gets in trouble, the other helps. If something's hunting them, one hides while the other runs out so the hunters chase it. That way, they don't get so tired or caught."

Carrie frowned. "You want to catch a coyote?"

"No, we're going to be the coyotes—that is, if you...well, I mean..."

"You want me to help?"

I nodded.

She didn't look happy. She scuffed her shoe on the sidewalk and looked at the pine trees. Then she looked back at me and nodded. "Okay."

I had Carrie spend the rest of the day getting the gate open to the Zooman's yard. I went to the hardware store and bought a new backpack and the rest of the stuff we needed. It took the last of my allowance money. When I got back, Carrie had broken the lock off the gate with her Dad's hammer. I looked at my watch. A little past five.

"You sure you can meet me here without your parents missing you?"

She nodded, then asked, "You sure we can't tell them?"

"Tell them what? That we've got to get rid of the Zooman's topiary before it eats someone?"

She rubbed her nose. "Okay, I guess not. But what if this doesn't work?"

"It's got to work! I know it's what the Zooman tried to tell that nurse."

I made myself eat something at dinner. Then I told Mom that I was going out to play. She told me to be home by nine. I wanted to be home long before then.

I didn't know if I'd ever come home at all.

Carrie met me out in front of the Zooman's house. We opened the gate and sat on the sidewalk, waiting. She didn't say anything. I didn't say anything. We just waited. I kept my hand closed on my new backpack.

Carrie looked up. "Sun's going down."

The streetlight over us flickered on, a blue-white light. It didn't seem very bright. Stars blinked on in the dark sky like someone had snapped them on.

Then I heard it. The rustling. The hair rose on the back of my neck. A breeze stirred Carrie's dark hair—and something else.

We both got to our feet. I looked at Carrie. "Ready?"

Staring at the open gate, she nodded.

Then a shadow moved out from the gate.

It moved faster than I thought it would. Branches rustling, limbs creaking, it came out. I thought it was the bear, but it had so many branches sticking out in so many places that I couldn't tell.

"Go!" I shouted at Carrie. We split up and ran down the street on opposite sides.

We couldn't run too fast. We had to keep the plant-things after us. My backpack slowed me down. I pulled out the first paper bag and poked a hole in it to let the bonemeal dribble out.

At the first corner, we stopped. I stood with my hands on my knees, the air sharp in my lungs. "Are they coming?" I asked.

Carrie nodded. Then she pointed.

I saw them, moving like the wind had blown them. The shapes blended with the lawns, with the hedge on the house next door to mine. I heard branches snapping against the pavement.

"Come on," I said, and turned to run.

Carrie started getting tired halfway to the hospital. "Don't stop," I yelled back at her.

She did. She looked behind, then sat down on the sidewalk. I ran back to her. "Get up. You can't stop here."

She shook her head and panted. "Can't... run...any...more..."

"Okay, then go up on the porch and sit real quiet. After they come past, you get to the hospital. Okay?"

She nodded and dragged herself up to the big house that I pointed at.

I waited on the sidewalk, listening, trying to see. My shadow looked thin and long under the streetlights. I heard rustling behind me and jumped. A cat came out of the bushes. I stamped my foot and shooed it away. When I turned around, I couldn't see anything moving.

I heard it first.

The soft "thwooping" like a branch being swung through the air. I ducked and felt something grab at my backpack. Fabric tore. I fell to the ground and felt a cold wind on my face. Then it was gone. I looked up.

The other plant-things were ten feet away and moving fast. Leaves shimmered in the light as they moved . . . first a front leg, then a back, then another front. Leafy heads bobbing, they snuffled closer. I waited and counted to three. I had to get them real close. I didn't want them to see Carrie.

My heart hammered inside me, making me sick. I waited. Just as the bear-thing stood up over me, I turned and ran.

They followed.

I ran until I thought my chest would burst. I ran until I thought I would fall down. I ran until I couldn't breathe. Then I stopped. I could still hear them behind me.

The hospital, with the woods behind it, was in front of me. Almost there, I told myself. I started running, but it was more like staggering.

Where was Carrie? She was supposed to be here. Had she changed her mind and gone home?

Leaning against a car, I looked around the parking lot. She had to be here. I couldn't run anymore. Someone had to get them to the woods. I needed to rest or they would catch me. I leaned over, hands on my knees, pulling in long gasps of air.

"Warren?"

Looking up, I saw Carrie. She had made it! While I had taken the plant-things the long way here, she'd come straight.

"Get them to the woods." I gulped down more air. "That's what the Zooman tried to say... wood! Go... wood!"

I pulled off my backpack and gave the second paper bag to Carrie. I had one more. "If any of them get too close, throw this away from you and run the other way." She nodded.

I was too tired to do more than sink down behind one of the cars. Five minutes, I thought. Just five minutes to catch my breath. I hated letting Carrie go out on her own, but I was beat. I'd only slow her down now.

Hiding was worse than running. I kept thinking that I heard leaves moving, branches snapping. I kept picturing the bear-thing leaning over the car and swiping at me with its paw. When I got my breath, I got up. My legs shook, they were so tired. I started toward the woods.

A round moon rose behind me. My feet hit dirt, not pavement, and skidded. Pine trees—dark, whispering trees that looked like just trees—made a black wall in front of me. At least they stay in the ground, I thought.

I ran, tripping over rocks. I fell once, scraping my palms on the dirt. Getting up, I looked around. I couldn't see anything but shadows. The wind whistled through the pines. Then I heard another sound. The sound of a branch whooshing through the air.

The lion-thing's cut stumps hit me square in the back. I fell, landing face in the dirt. I pulled myself up and turned around.

It hung in front of the moon for an instant, its leaves so thick that its wings looked solid. It opened its mouth and the sound of leaves being shaken in a strong wind was so loud that I had to cover my ears.

Then it disappeared into the night sky.

The winged lion hadn't gone into the woods

yet. It was still loose. I pulled off my backpack.

Instead of the third sack of bonemeal, I saw a ragged tear down the side. I stuck my hand inside the backpack and found my pocket light. Then I threw down the backpack and got to my knees. Feeling more than looking, I tried to find the third bag.

I could hear the lion-thing as it turned to come back. I searched faster. My hands brushed against rocks and dirt. I didn't have time to turn on my light. The whooshing got louder. Leaves rustled above me.

I dove against the dirt, but it knew that move. It dove lower. Something wrapped around my jacket. I felt myself being pulled up. Twisting, I struggled with my zipper. I got it open and my arms slipped out of my jacket just as my feet left the ground. I felt and crouched down as I hit the ground. How far away had it pulled me? Sweat trickled down my face. Next time, it would know to grab more than fabric. Next time, its branch-claws would sink deep.

Brushing the hair and sweat away from my eyes, I searched. The bag had to be here!

I heard whooshing, the sound of leaves in a wind.

55

My fingers closed over paper. I didn't care if it was an old newspaper, it was something. I turned and threw it at the same time. My back thudded onto the ground. The bag sailed across the face of the moon and into the woods. I saw wings blot out the moon. I waited. Then the wings tilted and banked. The lion-thing flew into the trees.

"Warren? Warren?"

I heard Carrie calling and slowly sat up.

Gravel crunched and then she was standing next to me. I got up, feeling sore everywhere. I started walking toward the woods. Then I turned and looked at Carrie. "If you hear me yell or anything, run. I have to make sure this works."

The moonlight made everything black or white. Struggling with my pocket light, I flicked it on. It didn't light so I banged it. A wobbly beam of light came on.

Pine needles crunched underfoot. I tried to be quiet. I could hear wood creaking in front of me. I walked toward it, my hands shaking so that the light jumped around.

They were all standing around a clearing, swaying with the other trees. Even the winged lion-thing was there. I knelt down and watched. Roots sank into the ground. Branches burrowed like gophers. The plant animals twisted and turned and, as they did, their shapes changed. They turned boxy, square, round-edged and into any shapes but animals. The creaking stopped. The digging ended. I listened as an owl hooted. This time when the wind rustled the leaves, I only heard leaves. And the sigh of the pine trees.

I sighed too, got up and left.

Carrie was waiting for me after school the next day in front of her house. She looked up at me but didn't smile. "I'm grounded for two weeks!"

I sat down on the curb beside her, and winced as I did. My muscles still felt sore. "Hey, I told you not to tell them where we'd been."

I looked up as a car pulled up in front of the Zooman's house. Carrie and I looked at each other. We both got up and walked across the street.

The nurse helped the Zooman out from the car. He had a big cane and still looked real thin, but the purple bruise on his face had disappeared. I nudged Carrie and grinned.

"What's he going to say when he sees his

yard?" she whispered.

We both watched as the Zooman leaned on his cane and walked toward his house. He stopped at the gate, staring into the yard. He looked as if he had never seen the place before. He turned to the nurse. "Do I live here?"

She nodded.

He looked at his house. "What a poor gardener I am. It's odd, but I dreamed about plants in the hospital, only I don't seem to have any." He started forward again, then stopped and looked at Carrie and me. "Hello, do I know you? I'm Mr. Hoffman."

Carrie skipped forward. "Hi. I'm Carrie. And this is my friend Warren." She waved for me to come forward.

I hung back for a second, unsure about it. Then I stepped up to shake the hand Mr. Hoffman held out. "Hi. Y'know, we can clean up your yard if you want. There's not much else to do in a boring town like this."

Carrie giggled.

I didn't. I was looking forward to living in a boring town!

WHO AM I?

by Roy Nemerson

1

I opened my eyes and sat up in my bed. I stretched and yawned.

OWW! My left shoulder hurt! I rubbed it, and looked at my wall clock.

7:25 A.M.? Why had Mom and Dad let me sleep so late? I'd be late for school! I jumped out of bed and headed for the bathroom. I checked out my shoulder in the mirror. It was deeply bruised, black-and-blue. How had this happened? During football practice yesterday? Did I fall off my bike recently? I couldn't remember hurting it.

I was still thinking about my shoulder as I headed downstairs. Mom, Dad and my ten-year old sister Margie were having breakfast at the table.

I pulled up short. My chair was missing! My place wasn't even set.

"Very funny," I said, staring at my empty spot. "Marg, is this one of your little jokes? Where'd you put my chair?" My sister and I were always pulling pranks on each other. "Come on, it's not funny, I'm going to be late for school—"

I suddenly realized how quiet the room had gotten. I turned to face my parents and sister.

Dad was rising out of his chair. Mom had moved to stand behind Margie. As if she were protecting my little sister! And all three of them were staring at me as if I were...a total stranger!

"Uh, what's going on here?" I started to say.

"That's what we'd like to know, young man," my dad interrupted angrily. And he sounded pretty serious.

I paused, blinked, and tried a little smile. "Well, for starters," I said, "what happened to my chair?"

My mother leaned over and whispered in

Margie's ear. "Honey, go up to your room and stay there until Mommy and Daddy come get you."

"Is he a bad man, Mommy?" Margie asked, pointing at me.

"Yeah, I'm a real bad guy, Marg," I said, making a face at her. "It's Larry Nicks, monster man!"

"Margie, go, now!" Mom said, and Margie scooted from her chair and out of the kitchen.

Dad turned and stared at me. I'd never seen him look so stern. His eyes riveted on mine.

"Okay, young man," he said. "We don't want— or expect—any trouble. You leave this house right now, walk out that front door, and we'll forget this ever happened. Otherwise—"

"Otherwise? Dad, what are you talking about?"

"Otherwise," Mom said, finishing for Dad, "we'll have to consider calling the police. And please stop calling us 'Mom' and 'Dad.' We're not your parents and we never heard of a Larry Nicks!"

"Okay." I shrugged. "Whatever you say." I had to admit this was the best family joke yet. But I'd have to wait until later to see the payoff. Because it was now 7:45, which meant first bell was just fifteen minutes away.

"I can't believe I'm going to miss breakfast," I said, heading for the kitchen door. "I'll grab an apple in the school cafeteria between first and second periods."

I stopped at the book rack near the door to grab my school book bag. It wasn't there. Another joke?

"Okay, fun's fun," I said, "but where's my book bag?"

"Young man, you're supposed to be leaving, remember?" Dad said.

"Dad, I can't go to school without my books!"

"That's it, I'm going to call the police," Mom said, heading for the kitchen phone.

If I didn't leave right now, I'd be late. I knew I could share a classmate's books for one day.

"Okay, I'm going," I said. "My best to the Leeds Police Department. Ask for Sergeant Collins, he helped me on a school project last spring. Have a nice day, everyone."

The walk down to Leeds Junior High, where I was a seventh-grader, usually took me ten minutes. Because of this morning's "prank", I was going to have to make it in under seven.

Boy, I had never seen my parents act like that before. Was today April Fool's Day? Hardly, it was the middle of October. What could they possibly be up to?

Well, I'd have to wait until that evening to find out. I had a full day of classes and then two hours of football practice ahead of me first. We had a big game coming up and as the team's leading pass receiver I had a lot of work.

I was thinking about all this when a minivan pulled up to the stop sign. I recognized the van right away. It belonged to Coach Herricks, my football coach. If he gave me a lift I could be at school in two minutes.

"Hey, Coach Herricks!" I called out, waving.

It was a mild day and his front window was open. He heard me and looked over. Coach Herricks was not only a good coach, but a great guy. Always willing and ready to help his kids.

"Could you give me a lift? I'm a little late."

To my complete surprise, Coach Herricks stared at me for a couple of seconds. There was no look of recognition in his eyes. His usual smile was missing. And before I could call out again he stepped on the gas and kept going.

I watched, baffled, as the van disappeared

down the road, toward the school in the distance.

I reached the school grounds several minutes later. Kids were gathered around on the front steps, waiting for the first bell, before heading inside. I'd lived in Leeds all my life, and this was probably my favorite time of the school year. The weather, the football season, being with all my friends—it was great.

I saw Kenny Brown on the upper steps. Kenny was the quarterback on the school team, and probably my best friend.

He was talking to several of our friends, including Joan Jensen, who was the head cheerleader. Kenny must have said something funny because everyone was laughing.

"Hey, guys!" I called out, as I ran up the steps.

No one looked at me. Kenny kept talking.

"We're gonna kill Hamilton on Saturday," Kenny said. "Even if our pass receivers aren't as good as theirs, we're still gonna beat them."

Pass receivers aren't as good as theirs? Why was Kenny putting me down? I was as good as any of Hamilton's receivers!

"Kenny, I've scored eight touchdowns this year. I don't think that's so bad," I said.

For the first time the group turned and looked

at me, Kenny, Joan, several of our other very close friends.

I waited for Kenny to say something. The group kept staring at me. It was beginning to make me a little nervous.

"Well, somebody say something," I said.

"Okay, I'll say something," Kenny said. He took a step closer to me and looked right into my eyes. Something about the way he looked at me sent a slight chill up my spine.

"You seem to know who we are," Kenny said. "So that leaves just one question...who are *you*?"

2

I burst out laughing. I couldn't help it.

"Oh great," I said, "you're all in on it!"

"In on what?" Joan asked. "Who is this guy?"

From the look on her face, you'd almost think Joan—and the others—really didn't know who I was.

I turned to Kenny. "Hey, Ken, listen, as part of this joke they hid my book bag at home. So in English and Biology classes let me borrow yours if I need them, okay?"

Kenny made a funny face and took a step back. "What?" he started to say, but he was cut off as the school bell rang.

Instantly everyone began moving into the school building. My first stop would be homeroom class, on the second floor. As I headed for the stairs I passed one of my oldest friends, Art Larson.

"Hi, Art," I said, as we passed. He looked at me and frowned, and he kept going.

"Art?" I said, "something wrong? Can't you say hello?"

Art glanced back at me. He was still frowning.

"Okay," he called back. "Hello. Whoever you are." And he disappeared down the stairs.

Whoever you are? Terrific, I thought, as I stopped at the top of the stairs. It looked like the whole seventh grade was in on the joke.

Kids were moving past me, rushing to get to their homerooms before the late bell rang. I realized I'd better do the same, joke or no joke.

I walked into Room 203. I headed for my seat/desk in the next-to-last row, by the window. When I got there I saw Joe Lemon was sitting in my seat.

"Uh, Joe, I think you're in the wrong seat," I said, standing by the desk. Joe was a real big kid, and not the friendly type. He was doodling in his notebook.

Joe looked up. He squinted at me for several seconds. Then he slowly stood up. Joe was a good four inches taller than I am. He was practically in my face as he slowly growled, "What... did... you... say... to... me?"

I felt my throat going a little dry. And my shoulder began to start aching again.

"I said you're in my seat. You sit one seat behind me. It's no big deal, but would you mind moving so I can sit in my seat?"

"Who is this guy?" Joe asked, looking around at the other kids, who were staring at us now. Most of the kids shrugged, a couple giggled.

I was starting to get annoyed. Jokes are okay at home and outside the classroom. But the school day had started. This was different. Besides, Joe Lemon was no friend of mine. Why had he been allowed in on the joke? I didn't even like the guy.

"Look, Joe, I know all about the joke, but right now all I want is to sit in my seat. So why don't you move back to yours—"

At that moment the late bell rang, and Mrs. Fisher, our homeroom teacher, called for order.

"Okay, everyone, in your seats," she said. She looked toward the rear. Joe sat down in my seat. I was left standing next to the desk.

"What's going on back there?" Mrs. Fisher asked.

"Mrs. Fisher, Joe Lemon's sitting in my seat and he won't move," I said.

Mrs. Fisher was a real no-nonsense type. I knew this problem would be solved quickly.

"And exactly who are you, young man?" she said.

I looked around. It took me several seconds to realize she was talking to me. "Who am *I*?" I said, my voice rising slightly. Mrs. Fisher had been my homeroom teacher since the fifth grade.

"Yes. Your name, please," she responded.

Mrs. Fisher was in on the joke! Boy, this was really something. Mrs. Fisher *never* joked around. I decided I'd better play along.

"My name is Larry Nicks, Mrs. Fisher."

Mrs. Fisher sat at her desk, and looked through some papers. Then she looked up at me.

"I don't have any notice from the head office of a new student being assigned to this homeroom. I suggest you go to the office on the main floor and ask them to check this out for you, Mr. Nicks," she said.

"Yes, ma'am," I said, and headed for the door. I passed by Rob Mitchell, who was seated near the front. He was the center on the football team.

"See you at practice today, Rob," I said. Rob looked back at me like I was from Mars.

The hallways were quiet now; all the kids were in their homerooms. As I went down the stairs I thought about what had happened since I'd awakened just an hour ago.

Everyone I knew, family and friends, teachers and coaches, were part of a big put-on. Why they had chosen me, I had no idea. And where it was going to head next, I also had no idea. But I was about to find out. The school front office was right ahead of me.

I entered the office, and saw Mrs. Porter sitting at her secretary's desk, working at the computer. Mrs. Porter had known me since I'd entered the Leeds school system in kindergarten.

"Hi, Mrs. Porter," I said. She looked up and smiled. I was already beginning to feel better.

"Good morning," she said. "What can I do for you?"

"Well, I don't know...this is kind of funny. First I guess I should ask—are you in on the joke?"

She stared at me. "Joke? What joke?"

All right! They hadn't gotten to Mrs. Porter. Good old Mrs. Porter was going to help me make sense out of all this.

"Well, beginning with my parents and everyone I've run into this morning, they're all pretending they don't know me. Mrs. Fisher even sent me down from my homeroom to see you about straightening out the matter. Pretty funny, huh?"

Mrs. Porter nodded. "I suppose it could be," she said. She looked at me. "What's your name?"

I stared at her. Had I heard right?

"Uh, Mrs. Porter, I thought you said you weren't in on the joke," I said.

"I'm not in on any joke," Mrs. Porter said. "But I can't help you if you don't tell me your name—"

"I'm Larry Nicks, Mrs. Porter, who did you think I am? I'm a seventh-grader, I'm in Homeroom 203, I'm on the football team—"

"There's no need to shout," Mrs. Porter said, as she started pushing keys on her computer.

"I'm just a little upset," I said. "First you said you weren't in on the joke, and now it turns out you are."

"Well, there is a joke being played here," Mrs. Porter said, staring at her computer screen. "But I think it's being played by you."

"What do you mean?" I asked.

"The computer file has no record of a Larry Nicks in the Leeds school district. Not now. Not ever."

3

For the first time I felt a slight sense of panic. "Computers aren't perfect, they make mistakes," I said, as I came around to her desk. I stared at the computer screen.

"See for yourself," Mrs. Porter said. "We have a Sarah Needham, she's in the eighth grade. Next, alphabetically, is John Nittles, a sixth-grader. There's no Nicks."

"Forget the computer, Mrs. Porter. Look at me—I'm Larry Nicks, 42 Bogard Avenue, you've known me almost all my life! Hasn't this joke gone far enough? I want to get back into class, I want my books back, and I want this nonsense to end!"

I was breathing hard, and my shoulder was really aching now. I didn't know what to do next. I was starting to feel like there was no one I could trust. Everyone was in on the joke. What was worse...I was beginning to doubt if this *was* a joke. But it had to be! How could I wake up one morning and suddenly no one in my life knows me!

"Uh, Larry..." someone said behind me.

I turned. I had been so deep in my thoughts I didn't realize Mrs. Porter had left the room and had now returned. Standing next to her was Mr. Lowe, the school psychologist. He gave all the students general tests, and was also there to help any kid who needed special counseling.

It was Mr. Lowe who had called my name.

"Yes, Mr. Lowe?" I said, sensing I might be facing a real danger here. Why had Mrs. Porter called the school psychologist?

"You know my name?" he said, sounding very surprised.

"Of course I do," I responded. "You're the school psychologist, you give all the intelligence tests."

"That's right," Mr. Lowe said. "And I'm also here to help young people who might be feeling a little . . . upset. Are you upset, Larry?"

"I'm *real* upset, Mr. Lowe. Everybody's claiming they don't know me. You'd be upset, too."

"Yes, yes, I understand. But, ah, Mrs. Porter says you claim to be a student here at Leeds Junior High. Larry, we both know that's not true."

Oh boy. Now they had the school psychologist trying to play mind games with me. I decided to fight back with my own logic.

"Mr. Lowe, if I'm not a student here, how is it I know everybody's name . . . including yours?"

"That's what we've been wondering, Larry," he responded, coolly. "How *do* you know our names? I'm familiar with a case upstate involving a young fellow, about your age. He so desperately wanted to attend a certain school that he memorized the names of all the faculty members and a number of the students. He ran away from home, and tried to attend this particular school. Of course, they found him out the very first day he tried to attend class. It was quite sad, really."

"You're saying I could be crazy and that I don't belong here."

"Not exactly," Mr. Lowe said softly. "But, Larry, sometimes we want something so much to be true or real that we let our imaginations take over—"

"Is it my imagination that I'm a starting member of this year's football team?" I blurted out. Mr. Lowe and Mrs. Porter looked at each other, then back at me.

"You're on the football team?" Mr. Lowe asked, his voice still calm and trying to be soothing.

"Yes, I am!" I said. "And the team photo's hanging on the wall, right outside this office."

"Then why don't we go have a look," Mr. Lowe said.

"Fine," I said.

It was still quiet and empty in the halls, but wouldn't be for long. The bell for the first class of the day would be ringing any minute. I headed straight for the team football photo, framed and hanging in the main hallway.

I stopped to look at this photo every day. I was so proud of it. I wasn't particularly big, so being a major part of the football team means a lot to me. I was in the front row, right between Rob Mitchell, the center, and my buddy, Kenny Brown, the quarterback.

"Okay, Mr. Lowe, if I'm not a student at Leeds Junior High, then how do you explain this—"

I stopped in mid-sentence. I looked at the photo. Rob Mitchell was in the front row. Standing right next to him was Kenny Brown. But I was gone. I wasn't in the photo!

Mr. Lowe peered in at the photo. "I don't see you, Larry. Where exactly are you standing?"

I took a step back. "They—they've doctored the photo. I'm on the team. I'm the starting right end! Ask anybody!"

"Larry, why don't you come with me, I think we need to talk further," Mr. Lowe said. He reached out his hand and placed it on my shoulder, the one that was aching.

"Ow!" I yelled, and ducked away from him. At that moment the bell rang for first class and suddenly the halls were filled with dozens of students moving quickly to their classrooms.

I was able to use the stream of students to get away from Mr. Lowe. I didn't know what Lowe had in mind, but I knew I wanted no part of it.

I also knew there was one faculty member who would never go along with this bizarre game. Mr. Hulbert, my Biology teacher. He was always teaching us about truth and knowledge, as well as Biology. I had to get to Mr. Hulbert.

Fortunately, Biology was my first class, so I scrambled down to where the Science department was. As I came around the corner I saw Mr. Lowe talking to a school custodian.

I ducked back quickly so they couldn't see me. My guess was Mr. Lowe was telling him to keep an eye out for me.

As soon as Mr. Lowe moved off and the custodian went away, I continued toward the classroom. The late bell had rung already, so everyone would be seated, ready for class.

The door was closed. I yanked it open and practically dove into the classroom.

"Mr. Hulbe—" I started to say, but the word caught in my throat.

Mr. Hulbert is slightly overweight, with thin white hair, and he's about my dad's age. But standing in front of the class was an entirely different teacher, a woman, maybe in her mid-twenties. She was lean, not too tall, and Asian, maybe Chinese.

She looked at me. "Can I help you? Why are you interrupting my class?"

"Where's Mr. Hulbert?" I asked.

"Who?" the woman said.

"Mr. Hulbert . . . he teaches this class!" I said.

"Hey, it's that nut we saw earlier, the one who claimed he was on the football team," came a voice from the middle of the room.

I looked over. Kenny Brown had said that!

"Kenny, c'mon, give me a break here, we're teammates," I shouted. "Did you know they've even cut me out of the team picture in the hallway?"

"Miss Lee, this guy's not playing with a full deck, whoever he is."

That was Joan Jensen. Joan! She was my study-partner in this class. How could she say something like that!

Miss Lee moved toward me. "I think you're in the wrong classroom, young man."

"I think he's on the wrong planet!" Kenny said. The class all laughed. I couldn't believe it. They were laughing at me like I was some sort of a clown, a joke!

"Go ahead, make fun!" I shouted, feeling my eyes starting to burn. "Who needs you guys anyway!" I turned to run down the hall.

"Oh, young man," Miss Lee said, softly. I turned back to look at her.

"What?" I asked.

"Don't you feel like a brand new person today?"

I was stunned. What was she talking about, I wanted to ask. But she smiled at me for maybe a second. And then, as if the wind blew it, the door to the classroom slammed in my face. I was standing alone in the hallway.

"There he is!" came a voice, shouting in my direction. I turned and looked. The custodian had spotted me. And suddenly he and Mr. Lowe were running right at me. I had to get away!

4

I was closer to the staircase than they were, so I ran quickly up the steps, taking them two at a time. In minutes I was back up on the main floor. And in seconds I was out the front door.

"Come back here! We won't hurt you, we want to help you!" Mr. Lowe yelled at me. He stood at the top of the steps at the school entrance, looking down at me.

I was all the way down the front steps now, heading for the street. I was off school grounds, so officially they couldn't come after me.

"I don't need any more help from you!" I shouted back. "If you wanted to help you'd put an end to this stupid joke! Maybe you all think it's funny, but I sure don't!"

"What joke?" said Mr. Lowe. "Honestly, I don't know what you're talking about."

His face and voice were so sincere. Was he putting on a big act like all the others? What bothered me was . . . what if it wasn't an act? What if they really didn't know me! But that was impossible . . . *wasn't it*?

I turned and ran until I approached Main Street. Leeds is a pretty small town. I paused to catch my breath.

I rubbed my shoulder. It was really aching now. I thought about Miss Lee. Something about her seemed so familiar. The more I thought about her, the more my shoulder seemed to ache. I'd seen her somewhere before . . . but where? . . . *where*?

"HaHaHaHa!" cackled loudly in my ear. I almost fell over, I was so startled. I turned around, and came eyeball to eyeball with Mac.

Mac was sort of the town bum. His breath always smelled funny. He was pretty harmless but he gave me the creeps anyway.

"You playin' hooky, kid?" he said, leaning in closer. His eyes were more red than white and it was obvious he hadn't taken a bath for a long time. His clothes were soiled and stained.

"N-no," I stammered. "I'm just, uh..." and my voice faded off. I'm not very good at lying. And the truth was, I *was* playing hooky.

"It's okay, kid, I won't tell anyone," Mac slurred. He held out a brown bag that contained something smelly. "Care for a little taste?"

"No!" I said, and I took a step back. I wanted to get away from this creep.

"You know what the hardest thing in this world is, kid?" Mac asked, his voice suddenly sounding clearer. I turned and looked back at him. His eyes seemed to glow, his body had stopped shaking.

"No, what?" I asked.

"Knowing who we really are. Yep. That's it. Do you know who you are, kid? Well, do you?" And he started to laugh like a madman again.

And suddenly I wasn't staring at Mac anymore. He had become Miss Lee! Dressed in Mac's rags, she was smiling at me!

"How's that bad shoulder, Larry?" she asked, her voice soft. She smiled at me. "I do hope you feel better real soon."

And she began to laugh gently. And then I was staring at Mac's face again! And he was laughing and coughing and his face was turning beet red. He kept laughing and pointing at me.

I turned and ran. I didn't even know where I was headed. There was an area of woods and open field just above Main Street, and there's where I ran. I kept going until I was sure no one could see me.

I reached a spot near the open field, and dropped down against a large tree. I don't know how long I'd been there, when I suddenly bolted awake.

I looked at my watch. 11:35! I must have fallen asleep. I rubbed my eyes to clear them. Ow! I had forgot about that shoulder. As I rubbed the bruised area, I looked around.

There was no one in sight. Just the large, open field, with the woods to my left and Main Street down below that.

My stomach rumbled. I had skipped breakfast and now it was almost lunchtime. Even with the weird events I'd gone through, I was still hungry. I needed to get something to eat.

I stood up. Maybe once I ate something I'd figure out the key to this puzzle. Maybe everything was actually okay now. Maybe if I went back to school it'd all be over, and everyone would know me again!

Sure, they'd all feel sorry for me now, and the joke would be over. I bet my parents and Margie were even waiting for me now, worried that I'd run off and they couldn't find me.

Feeling better about things, I dusted myself off and turned to head back to school.

"Larry Nicks!" a voice called out from behind me.

Never did two words sound better to me! The nightmare was definitely over. Everything *was* back to normal. I turned around to see who had called out my name.

Sergeant Collins, my friend from the Leeds Police Department, had come up behind me on his scooter.

"Hi, Sergeant Coll—" I started, but he quickly interrupted me.

"Put your hands against that tree and don't move!" he barked. And suddenly I was back to helpless confusion.

5

When Sergeant Collins was satisfied that I had no dangerous weapons on me, he turned me around to face him.

"Sergeant Collins, why did you do that?" I asked.

He looked at me. "How do you know my name?"

I stared at him. How did I know his name! "We worked together on that student safety campaign last term. Sergeant, it's me, Larry Nicks. You just called out *my* name!"

"I called out Larry Nicks because you fit the description of a boy using that name who was reported acting oddly at Leeds Junior High this morning."

"Fit the description? Of course, that's because it's me, and I wasn't acting odd, it's everyone else who's acting odd!"

"Oh, really?" said Collins. "You claim we worked together on a school safety program? The fact is until this very moment I've never seen you in my life."

I felt my knees start to buckle. I couldn't

believe even the police were part of the plot!

"Sergeant Collins," I said slowly, "the program involved how students should observe certain safety rules while riding their bikes, crossing streets, talking to strangers. Am I right?"

"Yes, that describes the program. But the students who assisted me were Kenny Brown and Joan Jensen."

"Kenny Brown had nothing to do with it!" I nearly screamed. "Joan and I worked with you!"

Collins narrowed his eyes and stared at me. "You have any identification on you?"

I didn't. I never carried a wallet to school, just my book bag and some lunch money. And today I didn't even have my book bag!

"No, not on me, but I do back home."

"Oh, yes, Mrs. Porter told us you claim to live at 42 Bogard Avenue. There is a Nicks family at that address, but we have no record of their having a son named Larry. And there's no one there to confirm or deny your identity."

"My parents both work in the city and my sister's a fourth-grader at Leeds Elementary."

"Look, young fella, you haven't really broken any laws. So I'm not going to take you in," Collins interrupted, clearly losing patience with me. "But I'm giving you a warning. You have no ID, you're claiming you're someone who doesn't exist, and you've been reported as a public nuisance," he said. "So here's the deal. If you're still in Leeds twenty-four hours from now, and I see you, you'd better be able to prove who you are. Is that clear?"

"Yes, sir," I said glumly, feeling more lost than ever.

"Good," he said. "See that you mean it. Because I sure do."

And he turned to hop back onto his scooter, and within seconds was on his way back toward Main Street.

I stared at Collins on his scooter as he quickly drove off. What did I do now? Was it really possible...that somehow...I had awakened this morning as...what had Miss Lee called me? A whole new person?

Could such a thing happen? No! It was impossible. I was Larry Nicks of 42 Bogard Avenue, and if Sergeant Collins or anyone wanted to see identification, I knew exactly where to find it. At Leeds General Hospital, where I was born, and where I knew they had all my birth records.

I quickly moved back through the woods and

soon came out onto Main Street. The hospital was about three blocks down.

I checked my watch. Nearly noon. I should be able to prove my identity by one o'clock, put an end to this stupid joke, make my last few classes, and then get to football practice at 3:30.

I walked carefully along Main. I didn't want to cause any suspicions. There were a few shoppers about, mostly young mothers and some of Leeds's elderly residents.

Elderly residents! I thought of old Mr. Jessup who owned the corner store where I bought candy nearly every day!

He didn't know any of us kids by name, but he knew exactly which candy each of us liked. You didn't even have to ask. Just walk in, and as soon as he saw you he'd have your candy on the counter. And he knew mine was chocolate covered raisins. I bought them from him at least five times a week.

I approached Jessup's Candy Store, which was just a block before the hospital. I glanced inside. It was nearly empty this time of day.

I went in. Mr. Jessup was sitting behind the counter. He had his reading glasses on and the morning paper in his lap.

He looked up and smiled at me. "Hello, young fella," he said. Nothing unusual about that. He always said that.

We stared at each other. I began to feel a little sick in my stomach. He didn't know me! I wanted to run out of the store, to race down Main Street, to shout and scream at the world: Stop it already, why are you torturing me like this?

"Want your usual?" he asked, with a big friendly smile.

I felt a warm glow. He knew me! They hadn't figured on Mr. Jessup in their little plan. He was just a candy store man, but he was the one who would help me. Mr. Jessup knew me!

"Yes, Mr. Jessup, my usual, please," I said, reaching into my pocket for fifty cents.

"You got it," he said. "Soon as you tell me what it is."

I froze. He *didn't* know me! I turned and ran.

6

I ran from Jessup's until I came to the hospital. There were several entrances. One was marked "Emergency." I felt like this was an emergency, but I knew I had to stay cool.

I walked into the Main Entrance instead. Several people were sitting in the waiting area. A few doctors and nurses moved about. I saw the Information Desk and went over.

A uniformed nurse was writing in a book as I approached.

"Excuse me," I said. "I was wondering if you could tell me where the records department is?"

"It's on the fourth floor, elevator on the right," she replied, looking up and staring at me.

As I waited for the elevator to come, I thought this was the first time I'd been in a hospital since I was born. I'd never been really sick in my life. I wanted to keep it that way.

The elevator door opened. I came face to face with Sergeant Collins. He was helping a man who had a cast on a broken arm.

"Thanks for your help, sergeant," the man said, "for getting me to the hospital and helping fight off those muggers."

"That's our job, Mr. Lane, to uphold the law," Collins replied. He said it to the man. But the whole time his eyes were on me.

"Excuse me," I said, as I squeezed past him to

get on the elevator.

"Having some sort of medical problem?" Collins asked me, as he moved abruptly out of the elevator.

"No," I replied calmly. "Just visiting an old sick friend."

Collins kept glaring at me.

"Twenty-four hours," he said, and the elevator door closed. I breathed a sigh of relief as the elevator moved up to the fourth floor. I was used to having the Leeds Police department as my friends. It was really no fun being thought of as a criminal!

The door opened, and I got out. I looked around. It was very quiet up here. The long halls were clean and brightly lit. I saw a directory on the wall.

It indicated "Hospital Records, Room 436." I moved off until I found the room. There was a closed door. I knocked and a voice from inside called, "Come in."

I entered. A man in a white coat sat behind a counter desk.

He looked bored. He was thumbing a sports magazine.

"Yes, what can I do for you?" he asked.

"I'm looking for some records," I said.

"What kind of records?"

"Uh, birth records."

"Whose?" he said, and for the first time he actually seemed interested in what I was saying. In fact, I felt uncomfortable because he was looking at me very intently now.

"My own," I said. "I'd like to see my birth records. My name's Larry Nicks—Lawrence Robert Nicks, actually. I was born February 17, 1981. In this hospital. I need the records."

"Well, that's no problem," he said.

"Great," I said, feeling relieved. I was afraid there might be a problem asking for them.

"No problem at all," he added. "Just come back with a parent or guardian who's over twenty-one and we'll show you the files," he said. He went back to his magazine.

"What?" I said. "Why?"

"Because it's a state law," he said. "No one can view or make copies of official birth records who's under twenty-one. End of discussion."

I stared at the guy. He was smug and rude, two things I really hate in people. But most of all he was keeping me from the one piece of information I really needed.

I noticed his name tag. "Beene, J.," it read.

"Okay, thanks for your help," I said. J. Beene grunted and didn't even look up.

I turned and walked out of the room. I took the elevator down to the Information Desk. A different nurse was on duty now. I tried to look as confident as I could. Inside I was shaking like a leaf.

"Excuse me," I said.

"Yes?" she said, looking at me.

"You have a Mr. Beene in Records?"

"Just a minute," she said, and she turned on a computer, hit a few buttons, looked at the screen. "Yes, James Beene. Records, Fourth Floor. Why?"

"One of the doctors asked me to tell you, they need him in the X-ray room right away."

She stared at me. "They need the guy from Records in X-ray? I never heard of that. Why?"

"I don't know. Maybe they need someone to take records of the X-rays," I said, not even knowing what I was saying.

She frowned for a moment, then shrugged, picked up her phone, and dialed some numbers. "Hello, Mr. Beene? This is the front desk. They want you in X-ray. I don't know why. Guess you'll find out when you get there. Okay."

She hung up. She looked around for me. But I was gone, into the elevator, heading back up to the fourth floor.

I had noticed there was no lock on the door to the Records Room, so I'd have no trouble getting into the room.

What I didn't know was how much time I had. I saw on the directory that X-ray was on the sixth floor. Beene would have to take an elevator up, ask for someone who needed him, find out he wasn't needed, and then take the elevator back down to four.

I figured this gave me three or four minutes, maximum.

I hid behind a door opening as I saw Beene leave the Records Room.

Beene waited for the elevator. As soon as he got in, I ducked into the Records Room. I went past Beene's desk. File cabinets were arranged by year. It took me several seconds to find 1981. I pulled on the file handle. It wouldn't open!

I noticed a keyhole on the cabinet. It needed a key! I looked around, breathing hard. Keys, keys, where were the keys? Beene must have the keys!

I ran back to his desk. Sure enough, there were several keychains in his desk drawer. I grabbed the first one. Each key had a year on it.

My pulse beating faster each second, I scrambled through the keys. My fingers were shaking slightly. A drop of sweat fell onto my shirt. There it was—1981! I turned and raced back to the back room.

Trying not to pass out—and I realized now I was on the verge of missing two meals—I put the key into the slot. I turned the key. The file opened.

The records were arranged in alphabetical order. I quickly went to the middle of the file, and found the "N's", where Nicks would be.

There was a noise out front! My heart almost jumped out of my chest. Could Beene be back so fast? I slowly moved my head around the file to look. Two doctors had stopped to talk in the hallway. They moved on. I breathed again, and returned to the file.

I scrambled through the N's. Each file had the name of the parents, and the name, weight, gender and time of birth of their baby.

I was talking softly to myself as I closed in on my file.

"Needman . . . Neufeld . . . Nibworth . . . Niles
. . . " I paused. Niles?

Shouldn't Nicks come before Niles? I carefully went back and did it again. My hands were
shaking now. Beene would be back any moment.
I had to find my file! And it had to be here, hos-
pitals didn't lose birth records!

I went through the entire listing for the letter
"N." There was no listing for Nicks born in 1981.
But I was born in this hospital in February of
1981! The records had to be here. So why weren't
they?

"Maybe what you're looking for's up in X-
ray?" came a voice.

I looked up. Beene was standing in the doorway, heading right for me.

7

I had to think fast. Beene was young and very
athletic-looking. And definitely stronger than
me.

I held up the file keys. "Beene, catch these!" I
called out. I suddenly tossed the keys toward a
wide open window.

"No!" Beene shouted. I made sure I tossed them up in a lazy arc so Beene would have a chance to catch them before they went out the window.

As Beene dove to catch the keys, I leaped over the desk and ran out of the room. I knew in moments he'd be on the phone and calling downstairs to alert them to what I had done.

I'd have to leave the hospital without their seeing me. I noticed a supply closet across the hall. I opened the door and saw an attendant's white uniform hanging on a hook. I grabbed it and put it on.

I took the elevator back down to the main floor. As I got off I saw a lot of commotion by the main desk. Nurse Lawrey was taking to Sergeant Collins.

"He was a teenager, dark hair, blue eyes, maybe five-foot-eight," I heard her say. She was describing me to Collins.

I saw Collins nod, and before he could turn around and spot me, I quickly headed off for the exit. I picked up a magazine and held it open, and up to my face, so people couldn't see me.

Then I walked out the front door, and as soon as I was back on Main Street I took off the uniform, and tossed it and the magazine onto the front lawn. Then I continued moving quickly down the street.

Where could I turn now? I was out of the hospital, but my problems had gotten worse. How could the hospital have no record of my birth? Had my parents been lying to me all these years? Was I born somewhere else? If so, why wouldn't they have told me? Maybe I was adopted. Maybe they didn't even know where I'd been born.

I was running out of maybes. I felt a panic growing in my stomach. Maybe I should just turn myself in to the authorities.

Because maybe I really *wasn't* Larry Nicks. Maybe I really was somebody else. Maybe I was like that kid Mr. Lowe had described, and was trying to be somebody I wasn't.

But if that were true, how did I wake up this morning in my own house? And how did I know and remember all these people even if they didn't know me?

And what scared me most of all, I realized, was I now no longer thought this was a joke. I knew it was something bigger, and much more dangerous.

WHO AM I?

There had to be something I could get my hands on to prove who I was. School was no help. The hospital was no help. Where could I turn?

"Of course!" I said, out loud. I'd go home! There were dozens of photographs there of me with Mom, Dad and Margie. And books with my name on them. All sorts of things to show who I am.

I looked at my watch. 1:30. Mom and Dad wouldn't be home for several hours, and Margie was still in school. I turned back up Main Street and toward home.

Suddenly the sky turned lantern-pink. Everything seemed to shudder, and somewhere, loud, throbbing music was playing. Strange music, not like anything on the radio.

I staggered back against a storefront. I was the only person on Main Street! The sky was changing color every other second. Pink. Yellow. Orange. Blue. Pink.

My shoulder started to ache its worst yet. I turned toward the store window I was leaning against, hoping for relief. Hoping for help. I looked into the window. And standing in the window, in a shiny black dress, smiling at me— was Miss Lee!

"What do you want? Who are you?" I shouted.

And suddenly everything had returned to normal. Main Street was its usual quiet self.

I turned to look at the window where I had seen—or thought I'd seen—Miss Lee. It was a new Chinese restaurant that had opened recently, and specialized in low-priced, fast-food dishes.

Miss Lee was nowhere in sight now. In fact, judging from the dark window, it looked like they weren't yet open for business.

I looked up the street. I saw a Leeds Police car slowly moving my way. Sergeant Collins might be looking for me after the hospital incident.

I decided I better get going.

I ducked into an alley and ran toward the woods behind Main Street. I'd have to run across the field and up one steep hill to get to our house this way.

It was a longer route, and my shoulder was killing me, and I was beyond hunger now. But it was the safest way to go, if I didn't want Collins to see me.

Ten minutes later I was standing in front of our house. I looked around and saw none of our neighbors in sight.

I was about to put my key into the front door lock when Mrs. Burton, our next-door neighbor, came out her front door, with a plastic garbage bag.

"Hi, Mrs. Burton!" I called out cheerfully. I was trying to think of a good reason to give her why I was home from school so early.

But then came the look I had come to know so well these past few hours. She stared at me and frowned.

"Uh, hello," she said, her voice filled with puzzlement. "Do I know you?"

I didn't know what to say. Were we playing games? Was I losing my mind? Was it something else? How should I answer her?

I decided to play it safe. "Well, I'm very close to the Nicks family," I said. "They asked me to drop by and pick up some things for them."

That didn't make much sense but it was all I could think of at the moment. And considering the last few hours, that I could think at all was a wonder.

"Oh," she said, but she didn't sound too convinced. She started to head for the disposal bin near the garage when she suddenly turned back and looked at me.

"Excuse me," she said. "How do you know my name?"

I stared at her for a full second. My eyes searched desperately for an answer. I spotted their mailbox. I pointed to it.

"Your name's right there. Burton. I figured it was you," I said.

She stared at the box, then back at me. She nodded, gave me a faint smile. Then she placed her bag in the bin and without looking back went into the house.

I breathed again, and placed my key in the lock. I turned it. It didn't open. My key didn't open the front door lock. How was that possible? It had always worked, why didn't it work now?

Had my parents changed the locks to keep me out? Could that be possible? Or was this another sign that I was suddenly a stranger, an outcast from my own home?

I had to get into the house. It held the answers to what I needed. I couldn't break a window, Mrs. Burton would hear it and probably call the police.

A window! Yes, the basement window in the back had been broken for the past six months. Dad had vowed to fix it, but still hadn't. Or, at least, I hoped he hadn't.

I ran to the back of the house. The window was still broken. It was a tight fit, but I was able to squeeze myself through and jump down into the basement. I was in!

First I ran up into the kitchen and fixed myself a baloney and cheese sandwich with lettuce and mustard. I washed it down with a half-quart of milk.

Just sitting in my own, familiar kitchen, eating Mom's good food, made me feel a little more secure. There's no place like home.

I glanced at the photo on the kitchen wall. It was from the family trip we took last summer to Los Angeles. It was shot by Dad, and it was of me, Mom and Margie on Santa Monica Beach.

I dropped my sandwich to the floor. I slowly stood up and walked toward the wall.

The photo showed Mom and Margie on the beach. But I was gone. I knew I had been there when they took the picture. I knew that. But now, just like the school football photo . . . I had disappeared. Vanished.

I felt dizzy, and held on to the wall for a few moments to regain my balance. I couldn't decide whether to cry or scream or what.

No, I had to keep cool, I kept telling myself. There had to be an answer to all this. And no matter what it was, I was determined to find it.

I went into the living room. Here the walls were filled with family photos. I was in many of them. I turned on the light, and walked to the large rear wall.

I stared at the photos. I was in none of them. There was a whole section Dad had put together, shots taken of me playing in football games, in uniform. Some of me making catches, others with my teammates.

The whole section was missing. Where the football photos had been, now there were photos of Margie playing peewee soccer, Mom on our sailboat, Mom and Dad with friends and relatives. Not one picture of me.

Relatives! I stumbled over to the phone on the desk. Maybe it was only in Leeds that I no longer existed. Maybe they still knew me in other places.

I picked up the phone and dialed my Uncle Ron's office in Chicago. Ron was my father's brother, and my favorite uncle. He visited us at least five times a year and always every Christmas holiday.

"Mr. Nicks's office," said the familiar voice of Uncle Ron's secretary, Miss Crane.

I paused for a moment. This was a major test. If Uncle Ron didn't know me, then I didn't know what I'd do.

"Is that Miss Crane?" I asked.

"Yes, it is," she said cheerfully.

"Miss Crane, this is Larry Nicks."

There was a pause on the other end. "Who?" she said.

"Larry Nicks. Ron's nephew...?" I felt my voice trailing off.

"Oh," she said. "You must be from a part of his family I'm not familiar with. Hold on a second, I'll get him for you."

My heart filled with dread. I'd spoken to Miss Crane maybe a hundred times over the years. And now she didn't know me.

A moment later the familiar booming voice of my Uncle Ron came on.

"Hello, this is Ron Nicks. Who am I speaking to?"

"Uncle Ron?" I said, barely above a whisper. I

was afraid of what I'd hear next.

"Speak up, please, I can't hear you," he said.

But I knew it was hopeless, pointless. My favorite uncle wouldn't know me. Would never have heard of me. And I couldn't bear to actually hear him say it.

"I'm sorry," I said. "I...I must have the wrong number."

And I hung up.

I sat silently at the desk for a few moments. And then I suddenly smashed my fist into the desk top.

"Who am I?" I shouted to the ceiling.

"Who? Will someone tell me, please! Because I think I'm going crazy! Crazy!"

I heard a key in a lock. And then the front door opening. Someone was home!

9

Who could it be? I looked at my watch. It was a little after 2 P.M. Dad should still be in the city. Mom didn't leave her shop until after 4. Had one of them come home to make sure the strange kid—me—wasn't there?

I heard footsteps, first in the main hall, then in the kitchen. And someone humming. Humming? Of course, today was Wednesday!

Mrs. Wesley came on Wednesdays to do some light housekeeping. She had been our housekeeper for years. And Mrs. Wesley always hummed.

There is no kinder, nicer human being on the planet than Mrs. Wesley. She would sooner cut off her own hand than see another person suffer.

If there was still any chance that I was the victim of some elaborate joke or hoax, then Mrs. Wesley would be the final test.

I went to the door and slowly opened it.

Mrs. Wesley, wearing pants, a sweater and an apron, was pulling some cleaning supplies from a large bag. She was humming what I thought was an old folk tune.

I didn't want to scare her. But I was scared myself. This was the most important moment in my life. And I had more at stake than I ever would in any football game.

I approached the kitchen carefully. Mrs. Wesley was spreading her supplies out on the kitchen table. She continued to hum the old tune.

"Mrs. Wesley," I said softly.

She let out a shriek and spun around to face me. Our eyes met. Her face turned even redder than it normally was. She started to say something, but suddenly her hands flew up to her chest.

"Mrs. Wesley! Are you all right?" I cried.

She gave no answer but suddenly let out a gasp, and fell to the floor. I rushed to her side. I lifted her wrist and felt her pulse. It was very faint and rapid. Mrs. Wesley was having a heart attack. And I had given it to her!

I ran to the phone and dialed Emergency 911. I told them to send an ambulance right away to 42 Bogard. Then I ran upstairs, found a pillow, and placed it under Mrs. Wesley's head.

Her eyes were closed. Her breathing was irregular. In the distance I could hear ambulance sirens approaching. Mrs. Wesley would soon be under medical care.

But I couldn't be there when they arrived. I had to leave.

I opened the front door and dashed outside. I started to run down Bogard Avenue. I passed the ambulance coming from the other direction.

"Take good care of Mrs. Wesley," I said. And I realized it had come out like a prayer.

I continued to run down Bogard, which led right back toward Main Street. I didn't know what else to do, where else to go.

I approached the school football field. Some of my teammates, including Rob Mitchell, were having a pre-practice catch.

I stopped to look at them. Suddenly one of them saw me. They all stopped playing and stared at me. Rob pointed at me. He said something, and the others all laughed.

"There's that crazy kid," is what he probably said.

I continued running toward Main Street. I didn't know why. But something was drawing me there. And I was surprised that even though I wasn't running fast or breathing hard, sweat was running down my cheeks.

And then I realized it wasn't sweat. I realized that for the first time since I was very little, I was crying.

I was crying and I wasn't ashamed at all. I was crying because whoever had done this terrible thing to me had won. Or maybe someone hadn't done it to me. Maybe I had done it to myself.

Maybe I had been bad sometime, somewhere,

and now I was being punished. But what had I done? And when would this end? Because I couldn't take much more.

I came over the final small rise and Main Street was in front of me. In just a few minutes the last bell would ring and the school day would end. A couple of hundred kids would suddenly be running, laughing, playing, heading home to their families.

But where would I go? I had memories of people who had no memory of me. I had no one, nothing to fall back on, nothing to go back to.

Maybe I should just go away from Leeds. Go to another town. No, that was crazy! I didn't want to leave!

I wanted my family back. I wanted my parents to know me and love me again. I wanted my little sister to laugh with me and not be afraid of me.

I wanted my friends to welcome me back and let me be part of their lives again.

I wanted to sit in biology class and see Mr. Hulbert again.

I wanted to be friends with Sergeant Collins again.

I wanted to walk into the candy store and

have old man Jessup know what my favorite candy was again.

And I wanted Mrs. Wesley to be all right again.

But I also realized if I couldn't prove who I was within a day, Sergeant Collins would have me arrested.

I looked up. I hadn't realized it but I'd walked clear down Main Street, all the way toward the far end of town.

I looked around. There wasn't another person in sight. Not on the street, not in any of the stores.

That was very odd. And it had suddenly gotten very quiet.

I heard the faint chiming of a bell. I turned. It was coming from that brand-new Chinese restaurant.

As I stared at the window of the restaurant, the chiming seemed to grow louder.

On very unsteady legs, I crossed Main Street to the restaurant. There was still no one around. Not even a car passed down the street.

Why was I feeling pulled to this restaurant? I wondered. Something about it seemed somehow familiar. But what? Why?

And just as I was about to turn away and move on, the bell chiming suddenly became ear-splitting.

I covered my ears and looked toward the window—and standing inside the window, smiling at me, was Miss Lee! And she signaled me to come near!

10

Like a magnet was pulling me in, I pressed up against the restaurant window. Miss Lee kept smiling at me.

"What is it! What do you want from me?" I shouted.

The bell chiming suddenly stopped. It was quiet enough to hear a pin drop. And there was still not another soul in sight.

"You know why you are here, Larry," Miss Lee said. At least I think she said it. I heard her voice, even though her lips never moved and she never stopped smiling, and she was standing on the other side of the pane of window glass.

"Larry?" I said. "Did you call me Larry?"

"It is time, Larry," she said. Again, I heard her

voice, but her lips didn't move. She kept smiling at me.

"Time for what?" I asked. "Time for this game to be over? Time for me to finally learn what's going on?"

"It is time for your fortune, Larry."

And she opened a white napkin. Cradled inside it was a fortune cookie. She dropped the napkin and held it up.

I looked at it. It looked like any fortune cookie you get at any Chinese restaurant anywhere in the world.

"That's what this is about?" I said. "A dumb little fortune cookie?"

"Watch, Larry," came the reply, as Miss Lee's voice filled my head. She cracked open the fortune cookie. It all seemed to be happening in slow motion.

I watched as the cookie part dropped to the floor. Miss Lee held the little piece of white paper. She looked at it and smiled. Then she looked back at me.

"Here is your fortune, Larry. Read it, Larry. Read it."

She held the piece of paper up to the glass window. The printing was small. It was hard to read. I couldn't make it out at first.

As I squinted to read it, there was a bell ringing off in the distance. The school day was over.

The fortune was blurry. I couldn't make it out. And then it came into sharp focus.

It said, "Starting today you are a brand-new person." A brand-new person! Hadn't she told me that before? What did that mean?

I looked at her. "What are you saying? Does this mean that I'm actually a brand-new person? How . . . how can that be?"

"We cannot escape our fortune, Larry," Miss Lee's voice said softly in my head. "And if we try, evil will come our way."

And then there was a flash of light, and she was gone. The window was dark again, and empty.

I turned back toward the street. Was that the answer? Was that my fortune, to become a brand-new person? But I didn't want that! I wanted to be the Larry Nicks I had always been.

"Afraid it's too late for that, Larry."

I turned. "Mr. Hulbert!" I cried. "Where have you been?"

"Waiting for you, Larry. It's time for you to become a brand-new person. It's time for the old Larry Nicks to . . . disappear." And he laughed

112

harshly.

"What? What do you mean?" I demanded. Then I looked up Main Street.

It was still silent but suddenly the street had filled with half the town. Everybody I knew. Walking. Up the street. Toward me. Silently.

They began to form a circle, coming closer to me. My mother. My father. My sister. My teammates, my friends, the people from the hospital, Mr. Jessup, Sergeant Collins, Mrs. Wesley (Mrs. Wesley?), Mrs. Burton, Mr. Lowe, Mrs. Porter, Coach Herricks, my Uncle Ron, and many more.

The circle was getting tighter, they were slowly, silently, advancing on me. I was trapped.

They were all smiling, they had their hands out now, reaching for me, about to reach me, almost touching me, and my shoulder was throbbing with pain and suddenly they all had the face of Miss Lee! And I screamed!

11

I sat bolt upright. I was back in my bed, in my bedroom.

My shoulder hurt like crazy. And I was

drenched in sweat.

I looked at my clock. It was 7:25 A.M.

Suddenly my parents burst into the room.

"Larry, Larry, you're awake, you're all right, thank goodness!" my mother said, rushing over and hugging me.

"How are you feeling, champ?" my dad asked. "Looks like the fever finally broke, just like the doctor said it would."

Fever? Doctor? I lay back on the pillow. I groaned as my shoulder continued to throb.

"That'll hurt for a few days. You had a nasty fall," my dad said.

"Mom, Dad . . . do me a favor . . . would you tell me what's going on here? I think I'm . . . missing . . . a few details . . ."

"What happened, dear," Mom said, "was after football practice yesterday you and Kenny Brown and Rob Mitchell and some of your other teammates stopped in at the new Chinese fast-food place on Main Street for a snack."

"Foo Ling?" I said, knowing what the answer would be.

"Yes," said Dad.

"Apparently you guys ordered some egg rolls, which came with a sauce. You dipped yours in the sauce, took two bites, and had an immediate allergic reaction."

"You passed out is what you did," Mom said. "And fell on your left shoulder, which is why it hurts so bad."

"They got an ambulance right away from Leeds General, but the doctor said there was no need to check you in, just take you home and you'd sleep it off. He said you might have a rough night, but you'd be fine in the morning."

Mom rubbed my brow, which was still damp. "Did you have a rough night? It looks as if you did."

I looked at her. "Mom," I said. "I have *never* felt better." And I gave her a big hug. "You have no idea!"

Mom laughed and hugged me back. "Well, you gave us quite a scare."

"I had a bit of a scare myself."

"Really, son? How so? You were out the whole time," Dad said.

"Let's put it this way, Dad. Allergic reactions to egg-roll sauce can create some pretty interesting dreams. My body may have been 'out' but my mind sure wasn't."

Dad nodded. "Well, the fever's broken. The

bad dreams are over. Welcome back to the real world, son."

"Thanks, Dad. It's good to be back." I was tired, but I'd never felt so happy in my life.

Dad checked his watch. "I must get to the office. You take it easy today, champ. And doc said no football until you're up to it."

"No argument there," I said, rubbing my shoulder.

Dad went out of the room, and Mom headed for the door.

"You get some more sleep and when you're feeling up to it, I'll make you some breakfast," Mom said. She stopped at the bedroom door and turned to face me.

"Oh, I almost forgot. The people from Foo Ling felt so bad about what happened, they've offered to pay all the medical expenses and want us to come back and have dinner on them anytime."

"Sounds good," I said. "Except next time I think I'll pass on the egg roll sauce."

"Yes," Mom agreed. "They're very nice people. They even sent over a get-well gift. It's here on your dresser."

Mom went out and closed the door behind her. I sat up and looked around. The whole thing had been a dream! But it had seemed so real, real enough that I hoped I never had one like it again.

I looked over at my dresser. Mom had left a white napkin on top. I wondered what my gift was.

I got slowly out of bed and went to the dresser.

I opened the napkin. Inside it was a fortune cookie.

I let the napkin fall to the floor. I held up the cookie. I cracked it open. The cookie part fell to the floor as I looked at the fortune.

It read, "Starting today you are a brand-new person." I felt my pulse quicken. I heard faint laughter. I looked straight into my bedroom mirror. I stared at my reflection.

And then I saw her. Smiling at me. For only a moment. But it was definitely her. Staring back at me, in my mirror, was the image of the smiling Miss Lee.

And then she was gone. And the laughter faded away.

I was afraid to move. I kept staring at myself in the mirror. Was the nightmare about to start for real? Would I walk out of this room and nobody know me?

I opened the bedroom door. Down below I could hear Mom and my sister Margie in the kitchen. They were talking; there was laughter.

I slowly went down the stairs. I was at the bottom now, at the entrance to the kitchen. I walked in. Mom and Margie stopped talking and looked at me. They both stared.

"Hi," I said.

There was a pause. Neither of them said anything.

And then Mom smiled.

"Feeling up to a little breakfast, dear?" she asked. And Margie came running over to give me a hug.

"You bet I am!" I said. And I took the fortune, which I was holding tightly in my hand, and tossed it into the wastebasket.

"Actually, I feel great, Mom," I said, and I smiled. I had almost said "like a brand-new person." But in fact I felt like the old Larry Nicks. And that was good enough for me!

CEMETERY SCHOOL

by Grace Williams

1

For the first time in my life, I was looking forward to the first day of school.

It was my first year at the brand-new Ivy Street Middle School. I was looking forward to some changes—a whole new school, a whole new year, maybe even a whole new me.

Oh yeah, did I mention my dad was the architect for the school? So I had a right to be excited; I figured I was allowed. After all, it's not every day that you get to start in a new school in a building that your dad just happened to design and build, okay? The whole town thought

119

the new Ivy Street Middle School was cool—it's totally futuristic—four floors and lots of glass and there's even carpeting in the hallways so you don't go deaf getting from one room to the other. It's even got solar panels for heating. And my dad was responsible for its being there.

He was the one that made it into something. He really cared about it—he told me he wanted to design a place where kids wanted to learn, not some dump of a cinderblock jail. And he did it, too. He even made the Board of Education and the city council give him special permission for some things—like all the windows. My dad says people need lots of natural light in order to think straight and without it kids won't learn as much.

So we were all pretty happy when it was finished. Without my dad, it would have been just a big hole in the ground right in the middle of Ivy Street, or just some dumb building that looked like a school, instead of like a space station.

It made me proud, knowing my dad could do stuff like that. Besides, it also made me feel like I had an edge, you know? Like I wasn't going to be just another geeky seventh-grader stumbling around trying to figure out where homeroom was. I knew where my homeroom was, and everything else, too. The blueprints of the building had been spread out over our dining room table for so many months, I had the whole place practically memorized before I walked in the door. So I was pretty confident. I figured seventh grade was going to be smooth sailing all the way.

Boy, was I wrong.

Now, when I think back on it, maybe it was just as well that I didn't know what I was getting into. It's like Lucille says, "Randy, you worry too much. That's the problem with the world today. Everybody wants to know the future. If people always knew what they were getting into, nobody would ever do anything!"

Lucille's my grandmother. She lives in Florida and tells fortunes with tarot cards and crystals. She moved there after she visited and liked the vibrations. Seriously, she moved two thousand miles on account of vibrations.

But that's Lucille for you. She's supposed to be psychic.

Not that I don't love her and everything—I do—a lot. It's just that she's, well, definitely not your ordinary cookie-baking grandma, with crinkly white hair and funny shoes. I'm not even sure what her hair color is. She's been a blonde, a brunette and a redhead since I've known her. Once, she even dyed it sort of purple. She said it was burgundy, but it was pretty purple as far as I could see.

Lucille says it's important to keep an open mind—to do things you never dreamed of doing. And that doesn't mean just changing the color of your hair, either. For Lucille, it's pretty much a way of life.

Like the vibrations thing. She told me once that if a person starts believing only in what they can see, it isn't very long before they start to see only what they believe. Oh yeah, and she wants everybody to call her Lucille, even if you're just a kid like me. She says it makes us more like equals, more like friends. She always tells me that I'm psychic like she is. Before, that psychic stuff always seemed kind of creepy to me. Now, after what happened at school—well—now I'm not so sure. Maybe I am and maybe I'm not.

It was on Sunday night that I had the dream. I mean, there I was, all excited about school the next day. I couldn't fall asleep. Mentally, I wandered around the Ivy Street Middle School, already knowing every turn of the wide, sunlit halls and before I knew it . . .

... Everything was changed. I could feel a tightness in my chest and I knew I was running, running as fast and hard as I could. The school wasn't filled with light anymore, like my dad had wanted. It was dark, terribly dark, and it was as if the darkness itself was made of something else, not just air. As though I were moving underwater, running from something at my back, something that wanted to suck all the light and the life out of everything. Even me. Especially me.

My footsteps echoed through the wide empty hallways and I could hear myself gasping, as though I'd been running a long, long time. At the same time, there was a howling coming from somewhere outside the big front windows, only it wasn't the wind at all. It was something like a voice or maybe it was a thousand voices, whispering all at once.

I dashed around a corner. I knew it was the right hallway, the one where my homeroom was. I thought if I could get inside, whatever was after me wouldn't be able to get me. That I would be safe. The light was on; I could see it, a dim yellow glow far down the hallway.

The thing behind me was closer now, I could hear it, feel it in the way the air blew warm on the back of my neck, like a breath. I ran down the hall toward the light with the last of my strength. I could make it—I had to make it.

I reached the door. The light was shining through the classroom window and I could see these figures dressed in black lab coats bent over a table, examining something, like doctors in an emergency room.

I reached for the knob, but it was sticky, slimy with something and when I raised my hand, it was covered in blood! And the thing was coming closer—shuffling down the hall. I looked to my right, but where there should have been another hallway and a stairwell, there was nothing.

I had to get in. The thing in the hall had me cornered. I pounded frantically on the window to get the attention of the people inside. I screamed and screamed, but there was no sound. One of the black figures turned slowly toward the window. But it had no face. It was just a bleached white skull, split in a wide, hideous grin. It raised its arm and beckoned me. Then all of them stood back—all those figures in black without faces moved aside to show the thing laid out on the examining table.

It was me.

2

My mouth was open in a long, soundless scream. I was bathed in a cold sweat, but at least I was awake. The nightmare hallways of the Ivy Street Middle School faded slowly away as I forced myself to check out the familiar things in my bedroom. Dresser, check. Bed, check. Dumb little kid spaceship wallpaper my mom had thought was cute about four years ago, check. Okay. I was cool, I was alive, I wasn't dreaming anymore. That was good. That was very good.

Slowly, my heart stopped pounding and I began to feel like I could take a deep breath without gagging.

As soon as I figured out I was awake and that it was just a dream and everything, I did my best to forget all about it. I mean it. I just lay there under the covers trying to think about stuff like basketball. The only problem was, I couldn't just forget it. The nightmare stayed with me. It was like it wasn't through with me, you know? It was like a bad taste in my mouth. A real bad taste. I felt like if I closed my eyes and went back to sleep, the dream would pick up right where it left off, that it would just go on and on.

Fortunately, my alarm clock went off just when it should have at a quarter to seven.

By the time I got dressed, I was pretty much back to normal. I was even working my way back to being excited about the first day of school. Except that at the last minute I changed my red rugby shirt for a blue one. The red made me think of that bloody doorknob in my dream, which made me think of the rest of it—those figures, that grinning skull—and the body on the table. Especially that.

I guess I was still thinking about it when I walked into the kitchen, because my mom noticed it right away.

"Morning, Randy. What's up?" She stood there at the counter, sipping coffee just as though she wasn't about to give me the third degree.

"Up?" I said, trying to play it cool.

She passed me a bowl for my cornflakes. "It's just that you look a little—I don't know—concerned. Something on your mind?"

"Where's Dad?" I asked. "I thought we were going to drive to school together today."

She shook her head slowly. "I'm sorry, Randy. They had some problem come up with the building and your father went down early to straighten it out. He was going to tell you himself, but you were already in the shower."

I glanced at her, frowning. "What sort of problem?" I asked.

Mom shrugged. "Some kind of leak or something. I don't know exactly. But you know your dad, he felt he had to go down and check it out personally."

"Yeah," I said. "Okay."

"You're not upset he couldn't drive you, are you?"

"Huh? Uh, no. No. The bus is fine. That's not it."

"What is it, Randy? Are you worried about something? You want to talk about it?"

I shook the flakes out in the bowl. On the one hand, I didn't really feel like spilling my guts to Mom about the nightmare.

But on the other hand, I thought that maybe telling her about my nightmare wouldn't be such a bad thing. Maybe it would make me feel less creepy about the whole deal. So I went for it. Told her the whole thing.

She let me finish. The truth was, once I said it all out loud, it didn't sound so bad. Well, it was still bad, but not *that* bad. It was more like hearing a scary story that happened to somebody else. When I finally got the nerve to look at her, she was smiling. Not laughing, just smiling, like she understood.

"You had an anxiety dream, Randy. You know what that means?"

"Sort of—"

"Well," Mom went on, "all it really means is that you're more nervous than you're willing to admit about starting school today. It is your first day in a new school, after all. Maybe you're even a little afraid."

Mom glanced at her watch. "Honey, I've got to run. But don't worry about it, okay? You're going to be just fine. After you get through this first day and everything turns out all right—you'll see, no more nightmares."

"Okay," I answered. She bent down and gave me a little kiss on the cheek, which made me squirm. I watched her as she gathered up her briefcase and car keys. "Bus in five minutes," she warned.

"I'm out of here." I was, too. I grabbed my stuff and beat her to the front door before she could get out of the driveway. She smiled and waved and I made sure I smiled back. It wasn't her fault I still had a weird feeling.

When the bus rolled up, the first thing I saw was my friend Eric's red hair, sticking up all over the place. His hair is the main reason you never lose him in a crowd. I've known Eric and his family pretty much my whole life. His mom and dad, his little brother, I've even met a couple of his aunts and cousins and stuff. And nobody else has hair like Eric.

Come to think of it, I don't think there's twelve other people on the whole planet Earth with hair like Eric's. He can cut it, wash it, plaster it down with hair stuff and it always looks the same. Bright red and sticking out all over the place.

Everybody calls him Eric the Red after some king who went around slaughtering hordes of people or something. You know—conquering countries and laying waste to the countryside. That kind of king. I think Eric likes his nickname.

The fact is, he pretty much has a personality to go with his hair. He's really great and everything, but way down deep, I think he'd probably like to go around leading an army and conquering people and laying waste to the surrounding landscape, wherever that is. We've been best friends since we were in preschool and I've seen him in action plenty of times, so I know. The guy is fearless. Totally.

I mean, if you sat him down and explained to him what being afraid actually felt like, he still wouldn't get it. He'd just clap you on the back and flash his huge grin and say, "Cool!" And then he'd get up and show you how he just learned to do something really dangerous, like triple wheelies on his skateboard in the middle of Main Street. Eric is like the brother I never had—but believe me—he's a little nuts. He just can't help himself.

So you can understand why I was a little weirded out when I saw him that morning. First, because he didn't look quite right. He had his usual huge grin and everything, but I figured he was a little pale or sick or something, because his freckles were even more orange than usual and he had these dark circles under his eyes. And second, because I was still thinking about that stupid dream. I really wanted to tell him about it, but like I said, Eric is not the kind of person who knows the meaning of the word anxiety. I didn't want him thinking I was some kind of wimp.

I made my way to his seat and hit him on the shoulder. "Hey man," I told him.

"Hey, yourself," he answered, punching me lightly in the stomach. "You ready for seventh grade yet, or is the bus dropping you back with the little kids at grade school?" He grinned wickedly, a challenge in his eyes.

"Funny," I answered. "I'm not the one who needed a math tutor all summer."

"Hey," Eric said. "I was never in any real danger of not passing math, okay? It was just a misunderstanding."

"Yeah, right." The real reason Eric almost flunked math last year was because he has an attention span of no longer than a nanosecond.

"I thought you were driving to school with your old man, the world-famous architect," Eric said.

"Yeah, me too. But he left early. There was a leak or something at the school."

Eric stared out of the window for a long moment. "Speaking of school, I got to tell you, I had the weirdest dream last night. About school, I mean."

Well, that got my attention.

Eric frowned, watching as the trees and lawns

went by. Two more turns and we would be on Ivy Street. "Yeah," he said. "I mean, it was weird. Weirder than weird."

"So tell me!"

He told me. And I listened, with this cold feeling in the pit of my stomach as Eric described *my* dream, the exact same dream—the dark halls, running from that thing you couldn't see toward the light in the classroom down the halls. I could feel the hairs standing up on the back of my neck when he got to the part about the hooded skull faces around the table.

"Eric! I had the same dream, man. Everything! This is too incredible. We had the exact same nightmare!"

Eric turned to face me. "The same dream?" he asked. "Even those creepy skeletons around the table?"

I nodded excitedly. "And when they stood aside to show you what was on the table, it was you, right?"

Eric looked away uneasily, snatching up his backpack from the floor. We got up to get off the bus.

"It was you, right?" I asked again.

When Eric's eyes met mine again, he looked

serious. Very serious. And there was something else, too. An expression I had never seen on my best friend's face in all the time I'd known him. He looked scared.

He took a deep breath. "No, Randy," he said. "It was you."

3

Eric and I filed in with all the other seventh, eighth, and ninth-graders into the huge front entrance of the Ivy Street Middle School. With all the usual first-day confusion going on around us, we didn't say anything more about the dream. I didn't really want to talk about it, if you want to know the truth. The sick feeling in the pit of my stomach was beginning to go away and I wanted to keep it that way.

I have to say, it all looked pretty normal. There was a big notice posted on the main door: that before the usual homeroom that morning, there was a general assembly in the auditorium, so we headed in that direction. I was pretty happy about that; after all the dream stuff, I wasn't real anxious to go to my homeroom, if you know what I mean.

Outside the auditorium, there was this big showcase that caught our attention. It was mostly glass and chrome with pin lights and lots of shelves and this gold plaque that said:

ARTIFACTS FROM THE SITE OF THE
IVY STREET MIDDLE SCHOOL

Only inside, there's all these really strange things. Things like a little kid's shoe from the olden days, the kind with buttons. And a long, curved-edged knife with the initials E.G. on the handle. There was a book that looked like it had been soaking in water for a hundred years or so, the pages all curly and moldy-looking. And a couple of rings. Stuff like that. It was just a bunch of old junk, you know? We stood there, just staring at this stuff for what seemed like a long time without saying anything. There's all these kids running around and yelling and trying to shove their way into the auditorium but Eric and I just stood there staring. Like zombies. I can't explain it. It was as if we didn't even know what it was we were looking at.

As we stood there, I could feel that cold sensation in my stomach again. I could tell Eric had it, too. Without even saying anything, without even looking at him, I could tell.

After a minute, Eric said: "Where did they get this stuff?"

"Beats me," I answered, "I think it's just a bunch of junk they found when they were digging the foundation. I'm not sure."

Eric frowned at the pieces inside the showcase, but his thoughts were somewhere else, somewhere far away. "It's like all stuff that belonged to dead people," he said.

I didn't answer him. I didn't need to. As far as I was concerned, he'd hit the nail on the head. Then the bell rang and broke the spell. We stopped staring and hurried into the auditorium, along with everybody else, and snagged a couple of seats in a row toward the back.

The assembly was pretty much what you might expect. The principal, Mr. McGivern, made this lame speech about how he hoped we would all rise to the challenge of the new school year with our hearts and our hopes high.

Eric and I rolled our eyes at each other as the applause died down. Then, the vice-principal, Mrs. Morrisey, began to talk about all the rules and regulations for lockers and the cafeteria and things that weren't permitted on school grounds, like skateboards and mountain bikes and Walkmans and stuff. Only right in the middle of it, there's this weird kind of wind howling through the microphone. At least, I thought it was the microphone. It sounded more like it was coming from everywhere at once, the walls, the floors. I glanced at Eric. I can't be sure, but I think his hair was standing up even more than usual.

The first time it happened, Mrs. Morrisey just thunks on the mike a couple of times. "Sorry," she says. "Apparently there are still a few problems with our new sound system."

Then she smiles at everybody, and goes on reading the rules like nothing happened. Then the howling starts again, louder this time, and about two hundred kids start snickering and shouting things like, "Hey! What did you say? We can't hear you!" Real mature.

The thing was, I would swear I saw her reach up then and switch off the mike altogether. But the wind just kept howling, louder and louder. So whatever the sound was, and wherever it was coming from, it wasn't the sound system. Besides, it was more like wind.

136

By this time, some of the kids are already on their feet, including Eric. So the principal just gives up and shouts for everybody to proceed directly to their first class, assembly is over.

My first class was World History, and Eric's was Computer Science, but thanks to me, we knew exactly where we were going. Like I told you, I practically had the whole place memorized. The assembly had cheered him up a lot, I could tell, by the way he was grinning.

"Did you hear that, man?" he asked as we rounded a corner. "That was really cool. Some billion-dollar sound system, huh? All blown at once, man." He started yelling and jumping up and down, imitating the sound that had howled through the auditorium.

Just then, I saw my dad walking toward us down the hall with two other men. One was wearing a hard hat and the other was some guy in a suit, whose glasses kept slipping down his nose as he tried to walk and read the blueprints he was holding at the same time.

Dad tried to smile when I got his attention and waved, but one look at his face told me something was up. He looked kind of worried. I can always tell when my father's worried. Eric was still howling down the hall and almost ran into the three of them.

"Hi, Dad," I said. "Don't mind Eric, he's just imitating the sound system in the auditorium."

"Yeah," Eric joined in enthusiastically. "It was blitzed."

The guy with the blueprint's eyebrows shot up. "Another problem?" he asked in a pip-squeaky voice. "Oh my—oh my—"

"It was like the place was haunted, man. Spooky." Eric giggled wickedly. That's another thing about Eric; he doesn't always know when to keep his mouth shut.

"Young man," my father said quietly. "I think you ought to keep in mind that a great many people put a lot of time and effort into building this school. You might want to think about that before you go making a lot of stupid jokes."

Eric was caught completely by surprise. "Hey!" he protested. "I didn't mean anything by it! I was just—"

But Dad wasn't listening. He turned to me. "And that goes for you, too. Now get to your class, both of you. I'm very busy."

With that, he was off down the hall with the

other two men, leaving me and Eric to stare at each other, stung into silence.

"What did I do?" Eric asked, offended.

But I didn't have time to answer. Just at that moment, the bell rang again to signal first period class and we scrambled down the hall.

I figured it was just as well I didn't have time to explain to Eric.

But when I thought of the worried look in my father's eyes that morning, I knew one thing.

Whatever the problem was with Ivy Street Middle School, it was bad. It was real bad.

4

When I got home after school, my dad was already there, waiting for me by the front door. He smiled a little when he saw me get off the bus and even waved at Eric as it pulled away from the curb. So I was pretty relieved.

He draped an arm around my shoulders as we headed through the front door toward the kitchen. Right away, he poured me a glass of milk and handed over a granola bar, without my even asking. So I knew he wanted to talk.

"Sorry we couldn't go to school together this morning, son," he said. "I got a call from the fore-man."

"I know," I answered. "Mom told me."

"And I hope you'll tell Eric I'm sorry if I was a little—uh, short with you boys there in the hall. I had a lot on my mind."

"No problem," I said. "You know Eric. It's not like he'll hold a grudge or anything."

My dad broke into a grin. "Well, that's cer-tainly true. But the truth is, Randy, there was a pretty serious set of circumstances at the school this morning. The foreman called and said there'd been a leak, but even I wasn't prepared for what we found."

"Bad, huh?"

Dad nodded. "One of the fourth-floor water pipes had broken completely. It totally flooded the bathroom up there."

"Bummer," I said sympathetically. I meant it, too. I mean, it must be awful when you get a huge project like the Ivy Street School all built and beautiful and everything and then stuff starts to go wrong with it.

"Bummer is right," Dad agreed. "But that wasn't all. If that broken pipe hadn't been discovered in time, the pressure would have affected the gas lines to the chemistry lab just below. You remember which room I'm talking about?"

I nodded. I could tell from the look on Dad's face that there was more.

"If it had gone unnoticed for two, or perhaps three more hours, the flood damage would have been one thing, but—"

"But?"

Dad paused and looked at his hands. "I don't even like to think about it. That school, full of children—you. It would have been a disaster."

"What?" I insisted. He was starting to scare me.

"If anyone had gone in and turned on one of the gas lines in there—a burner—it would have blown the whole school building sky-high."

I just looked at him for a minute or so, trying to sort out my thoughts. On the one hand, nothing had actually happened, everybody was safe, so no disaster. On the other hand, I was getting that creepy feeling again. That cold spot in my stomach.

"But how could a pipe break?" I asked him finally. "I mean, aren't they brand-new and everything?" I knew that even though he was quiet, he was mad—*really* mad.

"It didn't break, Randy. That's just it. We used plastic pipe in the construction, you know the kind I used in our bathroom upstairs when we remodeled? It's the best available."

"Sure," I answered. We still had about twelve miles of that same plastic pipe all over the basement. It was practically indestructible.

Dad sighed heavily. "It wasn't broken at all," he explained. "It had been cut. Deliberately. That bathroom was among the last rooms to be finished. Someone could have easily gotten in there and cut that pipe before the wall was up, and no one would have been the wiser until the water was turned on."

I just looked at him. The cold feeling had made its way from my stomach down my legs.

"That's not all," Dad went on. "There was that problem with the sound system. We were all over that equipment this morning and there was nothing wrong with it. Nothing."

My mind jumped back to Mrs. Morrisey switching off the microphone that morning.

"Now the whole thing has to be overhauled." Dad finished almost sadly. "Of course, every building has problems, but this—"

"This what?"

Dad looked at me like I was some sort of dense brain. "Well, Randy, isn't it obvious? Somebody is damaging the building—the school—as a prank. It's vandalism, pure and simple. Only I don't think whoever it is realizes just how serious the damage could be. People could have been killed. Now, I've spoken to Mr. McGivern about the possibility that someone at the school might be responsible. But I want you to be on the alert, too. Report anything suspicious to the school authorites. Okay?"

"Okay, Dad," I told him. "I will." I don't remember what I said after that. I don't even think it's really important, because I know I didn't say what I was really thinking. And I didn't say it because I was thinking that my dad was wrong about there being a vandal at the Ivy Street School. I mean, what he'd told me was perfectly sensible and all, but it hadn't made that feeling in my stomach go away. Without knowing how, or why, I just knew in my gut he was wrong.

Dead wrong.

5

The next morning, I told Eric my whole conversation with Dad. He was impressed, I could tell, from the way his eyes lit up when I got to the part about how the entire school could have blown up.

"Cool," he said enthusiastically.

I looked at him. "Cool? What kind of thing is that to say? Eric, this is serious, man. Every kid in school could have been blown into a zillion pieces!"

He grinned at the thought; he couldn't help himself. Like I told you, he's that sort of guy. It's not that he actually wanted horrible destructive things to happen. He just enjoyed imagining them. Eric has a pretty vivid imagination when it comes to blood and guts.

"Eric!"

"Okay, okay," Eric protested. "So your old man says there's a vandal at work. Somebody playing jokes and screwing up the equipment."

"Yeah, only maybe they don't know how bad it could get. Like that people could get killed, for instance."

Eric stared at me, his head tilted to the side. "Right," he answered sarcastically. "So tell me, Randy, how many vandals do you know who think ahead? Your average vandal isn't exactly considering the consequences of his actions. It's probably just some lamebrain who thinks flooding a bathroom or screwing up the sound system is funny."

"You think?" I looked at him. I guess I wanted him to tell me that's all it was. I wanted him to make that other feeling—the one in the pit of my stomach—go away.

But instead of laughing the whole thing off, he frowned. "Meaning?"

I took a deep breath. "Cutting that pipe, well, it's not exactly a kid-type thing to do. Even a ninth-grader. I mean, if you do something like that for a joke, you want somebody to see the joke, right? You want to hang out and watch 'em get sprayed with water or something. You don't hide it behind a wall."

Eric nodded. "I get it. But what about the assembly? That howling sound-system thing was pretty funny. And any tech-head can do stuff like that, easy."

He grinned, but it faded when I told him how

I'd seen Mrs. Morrisey switch off the mike.

"So you're saying all that howling stuff couldn't have come through the mike, because the mike was off?"

"Yeah. You got to admit, it's a little bit weird."

The bus pulled up in front of the school and slowed to a stop. I could feel my heart pounding wildly as we were filing out. Eric glanced back at me, his eyes full of unspoken questions. Whatever I was feeling, he was feeling it, too. I could tell.

"I got to admit," he said. "Weird is right. Only one thing to do, man."

"What's that?" I asked as we headed toward the front entrance.

"Check it out, of course. Investigate."

"Can't. Dad said it was closed up until Friday when they get the bricks replaced."

"So what's the matter with Friday?" He looked at me, challenging me with his eyes. "When's your last class?"

"Same as yours. Sixth period."

"Great. I'll meet you Friday at the fourth-floor bathroom at 3:20. Everybody's pretty much gone home by then, so it'll be pretty deserted. We'll have fifteen minutes to check it out, get outside and catch the last bus."

He grinned again, his eyes shining as he turned to jog off down the hall toward his homeroom. I don't want to sound like a wimp or anything, but I wasn't looking forward to hanging around after school on Friday to go look at that bathroom. I wasn't scared exactly, I just wasn't looking forward to what we might find up there.

That week seemed to last forever. Day by day the hours dragged by, before the last bell on Friday finally jangled through the building, sending streams of kids out on the lawn and into the sunshine for a weekend of freedom. I dawdled for a while at my locker, gathering up my homework assignments and jacket before heading upstairs to the fourth floor. My footsteps echoed crazily in the empty corridor.

As Eric had said, it was pretty deserted. I hoped that some teacher wasn't going to pop out of a classroom and ask me what I was doing up there. The truth was, I wasn't really sure.

But there wasn't anyone in the hall. Not even Eric. I thought he'd probably gone inside the bathroom already to make sure the coast was clear. My footsteps seemed to get louder and louder as I made my way toward the far end of the hallway, past the darkened classrooms. My hands began to sweat and I could feel my shirt sticking to my back under my jacket.

For a second, I considered forgetting the whole thing, turning around and running down the stairs as fast as I could go, but then there I was. The door to the bathroom was on my left. Just an ordinary door—nothing special about it. I pushed it open slowly.

The bathroom was divided into two parts. Boys on one side, girls on the other. You knew which side was which because they had these dumb little stick figures on the wall to point you in the right direction, just in case you happened to be in middle school and couldn't read yet. The boys' side was on the left, so I went that way first. Another swinging door led to where the sinks and toilets and stuff were and I tried to peer over it.

"Eric?" I said softly. "Are you in here, man?"

No answer, so I went inside and peeked under the stall doors. Nothing. I ran my hands over the wall behind the sinks to see if I could spot where the wall had been replaced. Still more nothing.

Then, I thought I heard a noise from the girls' side, so I headed out and yelled before I went through the swinging door. "Hey! Anybody in here?"

I mean, about the last thing I needed was to run into some girl in there and have to pretend I'd taken a wrong turn or something. But there was no answer this time, either, so I headed inside.

This was definitely where the leak had been. The cinderblocks they'd replaced above the sinks still hadn't been painted over. I ran my hands experimentally over the fresh bricks. That wall divided the girls' from the boys' bathrooms. Figuring in all the plumbing and pipes and bricks and stuff, I knew it had to be more than a foot thick. Probably closer to two. Again, the more I thought about it, the less sense it made that any kid cut that pipe.

I'm not sure about the rest of it—it all happened so fast. One minute I'm standing there, looking at these bricks and thinking, and then, it's like the whole room changed. The cold feeling hit me in the pit of my stomach like a punch.

Suddenly I knew somehow that I wasn't alone. Somebody or something was in there with me. Watching me.

The hair stood up on the back of my neck as I made myself look in the mirrors above the row of sinks. I saw my own face, staring back wildly at me, and I saw something else, too—something dark that flashed just out of sight when I looked up. I turned around, hearing my blood pounding in my ears, but whatever it was, was gone. My feet felt like lead as I dragged myself over to the toilet stalls.

I slammed them open, one by one, so scared I was angry. I think I was yelling. I'm not even sure. I guess I hoped it was Eric in there with me. When I got to the last stall, I slammed back the door and reeled away, covering my mouth and nose with my hand.

The stall was empty like all the others, the water in the toilet was clear and clean but a smell rose up all around me, worse than even the worst smell you could imagine in a bathroom. It smelled like something rotting and stinking and very, very dead.

I backed away, choking—not daring to breathe. I turned and ran as fast as I could, hurling myself through the swinging doors, past the stick figures and slammed hard through the hall door—

Smack into Eric.

I stood there, gasping and choking, still trying to get away from the sickening smell. Eric thumped me on the back and it wasn't until I got my breath again that I looked up at him and felt myself get mad all over again.

"You—" I said, still gasping. "You—where the heck were you?"

He stood there, his eyes big and his face pale. And suddenly I forgot about being mad. Because Eric was shaking uncontrollably. Because Eric the Red—Eric the fearless, looked like he was going to cry.

"Didn't you hear me?" he asked. "I was out here in the hall yelling like crazy for you. Pounding on the door. Why did you lock it, man?"

"Lock the door? I didn't lock the door!"

Eric grabbed me by the shoulder and hustled me toward the staircase, glancing desperately over his shoulder as we went. "That's why I was yelling," he said. "The door was locked, man. From the inside."

6

For the next few weeks, I did my best not to think about the bathroom incident. Or any of the rest of it either, the dream, that creepy feeling, anything. I concentrated on going to my classes and doing my homework and trying to pretend that everything was normal, like I didn't get a cold feeling in my stomach every time I went to the fourth floor, or that I wasn't scared to be alone in a hallway. It almost even worked.

I mean, it's pretty easy not to ever be alone when you spend your days in a building with a few hundred other people. I almost forgot how scared I'd been.

Eric tried to forget about it, too. I think he came a lot closer to actually forgetting than I did. I have to admit, there are times in a kid's life when having a short attention span can be a real advantage. A person can drive themselves nuts trying to figure out stuff like this, you know?

Sure, I suppose we ought to have told some-body what had gone on that Friday afternoon—you know, like an adult or something—but I honestly couldn't see the point. You tell somebody a story like that and they can't explain it, so instead they just pretend they don't believe you. Then they start asking a lot of nosey questions like what were you doing there in the first place when you should have been on the school bus? As if that made a difference.

Then, before you know it, they get the whole thing twisted around and they're making it seem like it was *your* fault that you were practically attacked by an unseen force and overwhelmed by supernatural noxious odors. They act like it's supposed to be your punishment for not having gotten on the school bus, which doesn't exactly help. I mean, what if I'd died or something? I can just see all these people around my funeral making really brilliant remarks like, "Too bad for Randy. He should have been on that school bus."

So we just kept our mouths shut. We figured it was the best thing to do. The weird thing was, as soon as we decided keep quiet, everybody else started talking. We began to hear all kinds of crazy rumors. Every day, some new story would sweep through the lunchroom or the locker room or get passed around in a note in English class.

Week after week, the stories got wilder. Jim

Ferguson told me that the faucets in the art room were leaking something that looked a lot like blood. Then, the next day, I heard from Dave Lafitte that it hadn't been blood at all, but that somebody had stuffed a bunch of red pigment way up into the spout, so it would just seem like it was blood.

Then, just as soon as that mystery looked like it had been solved, Eric heard from Taylor Morgan that somebody had snuck in and smeared smelly green slime all over the walls of the Biology room. The teacher dismissed the class and went to go tell someone, but by the time she came back, the slime was gone. Completely.

But after that, somebody else said the only reason they had a slime explosion in the first place was because somebody put MiracleGro in all the petri dishes.

A week or so later, we heard another story that somebody had found this eighth-grade girl locked inside her own locker overnight! When they finally got her out the next day, she was pretty hysterical, shrieking and crying and everything and saying that someone had pushed her inside after her violin lesson. Eric didn't believe that one, but way down deep, I think I did.

I mean, I figured a story like that has to be true. Nobody, but nobody, is dumb enough to lock themselves in their own locker.

Then, the second week of October, the school librarian claimed he'd been pushed off a ladder and broken his ankle. When he finally got up to call somebody, he found all the books torn off the library shelves—every last one. And that's when things really started to get bad.

The principal called a special assembly of the entire student body. He ran down the whole list of things that had happened since the Ivy Street Middle School had opened its doors. There was stuff I didn't even know about, like the athletic field. Every time they tried to put down new sod in the corner nearest the school, somebody would dig it all up. It's weird . . . did you ever notice how you can see something every day without *really* seeing it? I mean, I'd passed that corner of the field every day for a month and I noticed it was dug up and everything, but I never dreamed somebody was doing it on purpose!

There was other stuff, too. Like the ninth-grade boys' gym class that found all their gym shoes missing. All the lockers were still locked, but the shoes were gone. You know where they finally found the missing shoes? The bottom of the swimming pool.

Mr. McGivern finished up by asking for the culprit or culprits responsible to come forward and claim responsibility. And then he just let us sit there for maybe fifteen minutes waiting for something to happen. Only nothing did. Big surprise—nobody came forward.

After what seemed like a long time, Mr. McGivern finally spoke once more.

"Well," he said, "perhaps it was too much to ask that the person or persons responsible for these things own up to it. These vandals have done thousands of dollars' worth of damage to this school. They have frightened people and now someone has been hurt. Mr. Jones could even have been killed. And it is the fault of someone in this room. I promise him, and I promise you, this will not go unpunished. We will find you, whoever you are."

I kept glancing at the librarian all through the principal's speech. He wouldn't even look at anybody. He just kept staring at his hands, turning them over and over in his lap.

And then I knew that no kid had pushed him off that ladder.

I knew absolutely that Mr. Jones had tangled with the same force Eric and I met in the fourth-floor bathroom. Call it a gut feeling, call it ESP, but I knew it. I was so sure, I couldn't help smile—it made me think of my grandmother Lucille down there in Florida. Maybe she'd been right about my being psychic all along.

And suddenly I wished like anything she was sitting right beside me, there in the auditorium. If whatever it was could push a big guy like Mr. Jones off a ladder, I was suddenly pretty sure it could do worse. Much worse.

Even then, I really tried to be realistic. With all the stuff I'd just heard, you had to figure maybe there really was a vandal or prankster on the loose. It was the only logical explanation. But I looked again at Mr. Jones and I saw the miserable, frightened look on his face. And I knew that sometimes logic just isn't enough.

That's when Mr. McGivern brought out the big guns.

"As you know, boys and girls, it is now less than a week to Halloween. Traditionally, the parents and teachers of the Ivy Street School District have banded together to insure that everyone has a safe and enjoyable celebration."

A murmur swept through the crowd and the audience seemed to hold its breath. This was one time when you didn't need ESP to know what was coming.

"But Halloween is also a time for pranks and practical jokes. Given the trouble this school has experienced over the past few weeks, these pranks promise to get worse as Halloween approaches. I cannot allow that to happen. Therefore the PTA will contact your parents for their complete cooperation in seeing to it that all Halloween festivities are cancelled."

A giant groan of protest sounded. The principal held up his hand for silence. "In addition, there will be a three-hour general detention in this auditorium on Halloween. Everyone will be required to attend. When it is over, each student will then be personally escorted home by his or her parents or appointed guardians."

The groans turned into cries of protest. Mr. McGivern only nodded sadly as he waited for the hubbub to die down. "Until that time, school grounds will be patrolled by a uniformed security force. Any student found in the halls or on the grounds between classes or after classes without a written pass risks expulsion. Not suspension—

expulsion."

When we heard that, every kid in the place got totally quiet. Seriously, you could have heard a mouse breathe.

"It will seem as though I am punishing all of you for the acts of a few," Mr. McGivern continued. "That is not my intention. But I will not allow these pranks to go on when your safety is at risk. And I feel I cannot impress on you just how grave the situation really is. I am sorry this is how it has to be. Have a nice day. Dismissed."

I have to tell you, I don't think the guy gave himself enough credit. About not being able to impress on us how serious it was, I mean. I don't think there was a kid left in school who didn't know it was for real as we filed out of the auditorium that day.

For once, even Eric had nothing to say. I caught up with him just as he was leaving. He was truly bummed. Halloween is Eric's absolute favorite day. Better than Christmas even. I think it has something to do with the blood and monsters and stuff. He'd had his costume all planned for months. He was going as Attila the Hun. He wasn't going to go out trick-or-treating or any of that kid stuff, he was just going to answer the door and bellow and scare people. Only now, it looked like that definitely wasn't going to happen.

We stopped near the big showcase that stood outside the auditorium. I stood with my back to it as hordes of kids swarmed around us on their way to their next classes. "You can do Attila next year," I said in an attempt to make Eric feel a bit better.

"I got the horns glued on the helmet and everything," he answered miserably.

"Maybe they'll catch whoever it is," I told him. "Who knows? Maybe the whole detention thing won't even happen."

But Eric wasn't listening. Instead he was looking over my shoulder towards the glass showcase, his eyes wide. As I looked at him, my heart began to pound wildly. I remembered that first day when we'd both stood in the same spot, staring like zombies. I wanted to turn around, to see what he was seeing, but I couldn't; I was afraid. Eric's eyes were dark and wide with disbelief. All around us, kids were passing by, making their way down the hall.

My voice trembled a little, and I reached out to shake him by the shoulder. "Eric?" I said.

"What is it, man?"

He seemed to come back to himself all at once. He tore his eyes away from the case and looked at me like he was seeing me for the first time. "Turn around," he said.

I turned around. At first, I couldn't see anything but the same old junk that had been in there before. But then Eric shoved me a little to the left and pointed to a spot where the window of the case caught the light from above. And there, scratched deep in the glass in odd, jagged letters was written:

"Urs iz hours."

7

Looking back, it was unbelievable to think how stupid we were. No lie. I mean, now the words scratched in the glass of the showcase seem totally obvious. But at the time, what can I tell you? We just didn't get it. Neither of us. It's like I told you about seeing that corner of the athletic field all dug up every time I passed it. You know what you're seeing, okay? It's just that you can't always know what it means.

And then there was the fact that it didn't exactly turn out to be your ordinary day at school, either. First, there was the bad news about the Halloween detention we got at the assembly and then finding those words etched in the glass.

Then, there was lunch.

By the time lunchtime rolled around, the whole attitude of the Ivy Street Middle School had changed. For the worse. A lot of kids were mad about what they thought was unfair treatment, but just as many others were suspicious and afraid. You saw kids walking down the hall, crying for no reason. Two guys in my gym class got into a fistfight. Over nothing. Or at least, nothing you could see.

Most of the teachers got through the morning's classes without too much yelling, but they were edgy, too. You could feel it. It was as if something had been unleashed, something that stalked the corridors and filled into the classrooms.

It was something in the air and in the water and in the little bits of things you sometimes see out of the corner of your eye. It was everywhere and nowhere.

But by 12:30 or so, the cold feeling in my

gut was so bad I'd almost gotten used to it. And I knew deep down that somehow everything was different. Something was going to happen. Everyone could feel it. And everyone was hoping it would happen soon.

When I caught up with Eric in the cafeteria line at lunchtime, I could hardly stand the thought of eating. I grabbed a tray and slid into a line that seemed about a hundred kids long. I felt light-headed, almost as if I could pass out. Eric didn't look much better. His hand was shaking a little as he grabbed an apple and a carton of juice from the refrigerated section.

"How you doin', man?" he asked under his breath. "Is it just me, or is it kind of like a riot is about to break out in here?"

"No kidding," I answered, as the usual lunchtime noise levels rose to the pain level.

"You figure out those scratches yet?" Eric asked.

I snapped. I couldn't help it. "Why do I always have to figure everything out, Brillo head? You got a low IQ or something?"

He scowled at me and I could tell I'd hurt his feelings. I could tell I'd made him mad, really mad. Only I didn't care. It was like I'd fallen under the spell of the evil that had come to the Ivy Street School. It had me, too. And I didn't care. I wanted to hurt him—someone—everyone. I couldn't control it . . . and I didn't *want* to control it.

My breath was coming hard as we inched down the line toward the hot foods.

I could feel my sweaty hands slipping on my tray. I remember thinking that it was just going to be the usual slop that I couldn't stand anymore. I wished I could just get out of there and run away somewhere. Anywhere.

We edged further and the steam billowed up as the cafeteria workers spooned out portion after portion, plate after plate in an endless procession, their faces blank and expressionless. Like robots. Like zombies. I pointed to the macaroni and cheese and a portion plopped down on the plate that was passed to me.

And then the screaming began.

I snapped out of my evil trance to see a girl near the cashier, looking down at her plate and pointing and screaming and sobbing and tearing at her hair. And then everyone was screaming at once. I heard someone barf, in back of me, then someone else and someone else after that.

A teacher started screaming over and over for somebody to call 911. In an instant, Eric grabbed my tray out of my hands and flung it across the floor.

I stared at him dumbly, until he pointed a shaking finger at the tray of macaroni and cheese. And there, almost hidden among the elbows, swimming in the yellow-orange cheese sauce, I could see something moving, wriggling, squirming—no bigger than threads, some of them. No longer than your fingernail. But alive. Definitely alive.

8

I guess I don't have to tell you they cancelled school for the rest of the day. They called my mom at her office, and she came by to pick me up. Eric came with us. His dad was out of town and his mother had some appointment or something, so she said it was okay if Eric stayed with me. As we passed Mr. McGivern on the way out, he was trying to calm down this group of mothers all yelling at once. As if it was his fault. He was keeping his cool pretty well, but I had to feel sorry for the guy. For a principal, he had to be having a pretty lousy day.

Mom made a worried face as she swung out of the lot. "This is just terrible! I never heard of anything like this—" she kept saying.

"That's probably a good thing, Mom." I tried to be reassuring. "That probably means it doesn't happen too often."

"You boys all right? Should I call the doctor?"

"We're fine, Mom. Honestly."

Eric snickered a little and started to jam a finger down his throat in a pretend gag. So I quietly punched him in the stomach to make him stop.

As soon as we were alone, Eric opened the fridge and started to poke around inside. He found some chocolate syrup and poured about half of it over a carton of passion-fruit yogurt. I think it was safe to say the school lunch hadn't exactly affected his appetite.

I wasn't hungry. There was something I had to get off my chest. "Eric, man," I began. "Look, I'm uh, really sorry. About being mean to you in the cafeteria. And I want to thank you, you know, for getting rid of my tray and everything."

He peered up at me over the yogurt. "Hey, man, no sweat. The whole place was going nuts.

It's not like it was just you."

"But you're the one I yelled at—"

"Forget it, okay?" He smacked at the last spoonful of yogurt and licked his lips. "We got more important things to worry about anyhow. Like why a brand-new building like that is full of ghosts. That's the part I don't get."

I stared at him. "Ghosts?"

"Well, yeah. It's pretty obvious, isn't it? We already know it isn't some kid cutting plumbing pipes and digging up the athletic field and dumping worms in the Cheez Whiz. It can't be. First, because no kid I know is that smart and second, because there's no opportunity. If even two or three kids are responsible for all this stuff, they'd have to be the busiest kids on earth. Like digging up the playing field. That's gotta take hours, man. The whole night, every night."

"But why do you think the school is—well—"

"Haunted? Easy. It's like all those mystery shows on TV. In order to know who committed the crime, you figure who had the motive, then who had the means and last, who had the opportunity. You follow?"

I nodded.

"So," Eric went on. "No kid or even group of

kids is doing this. Rule that out. First, because there's no motive. When a kid plays a prank or a practical joke, it's for a reason. Like to get back at some other kid for something. You know, to make 'em look stupid. They don't go around trashing an entire building and getting Halloween cancelled. It doesn't make sense, because they get punished along with everybody else."

I nodded again. The truth was, I was pretty impressed with what Eric was saying. I mean, I'd been thinking along the same lines myself, but it made a difference somehow, hearing it out loud and logical, the way he had it.

"And then there's the problem with means. Some stuff a kid could do, like messing with the sound system or screwing up the faucets in art class, but a kid couldn't have done all of it. Like the digging or the worms. I mean, where do you go to buy worms?"

"A bait shop?" I suggested.

"For night crawlers, sure. But not for what we saw. I think it was some kind of larvae. You know any larvae shops in town?"

I had to admit he was right.

"So we know that kids don't have the motive and don't have the means. Which brings us to opportunity. Nobody has the time to be doing all this stuff. No way. Take those words on the showcase. Everybody in the entire school was at that assembly this morning. Everybody. Can you tell me someone snuck out and scratched that stuff in the glass without anyone seeing? Besides, those letters were scratched deep, real deep. To do that, you have to have something harder than glass, like a diamond. You know a kid with a diamond?"

"What if it's a grown-up?" I asked. "They could have the means and the opportunity."

"I thought about that, but I don't see a motive. I mean, there's no reason for an adult with no connection to the school to do any of this, and any parent with a kid in school doesn't want to close the place down. Parents want kids *in* school, not out."

I thought hard. "A teacher?" I suggested.

"Nah," Eric said, reaching into the cupboard for a box of cookies. "Too risky. Besides, you don't get to be a teacher if you're a psycho. They make you take a test."

"Right."

"Besides—" Eric paused and looked at me, chewing a cookie carefully, "in that cafeteria today, you saw what happened. It was like—I don't know. Like mass-hypnosis or something. Everybody went nuts, man. Even you, a little bit. You could feel it. How can a teacher do that?"

"You're right," I told him again. He was, too.

"It's like this, Randy. There's no natural explanation for what's been going on, so it must be something supernatural. Like aliens maybe. Or ghosts. I sort of wish it was aliens, but the way things are going, I figure it's got to be haunted. Only I can't figure out why."

I reached for a cookie.

"Hmm—I still don't get it, then. What kind of ghost would haunt a middle school?"

I didn't know. But we were about to find out. Because just at that moment the telephone rang, making us both jump. It was kind of creepy, to tell you the truth. I picked up the receiver.

It was Lucille, calling from Florida.

9

I was never so glad to hear from anybody in my life. "Hey, Lucille!" I said, grinning into the phone.

"Hey, yourself," she answered. "I've been thinking about you all day, Randy. Ever since this morning. Your vibrations have been very strong. Especially strong. Have you been thinking about me?"

I remembered the assembly that morning, and how I had wished she were there. "I sort of have," I told her. "But how come you're calling now? I mean, I'm usually in school at this hour."

Lucille gave an impatient little sigh. "Randy my boy, give your old grandma a little credit. I knew you'd be there, that's all. So I called."

"Well—" I began, but she interrupted me before I could finish.

"—and you're psychic, too. Even if you won't admit it. How do you think I knew you've been thinking about me?"

"I know, Lucille, but—"

"But nothing. So why are you home from school? You're not sick, are you? No, of course you're not. But someone is. I can sense it. Are a lot of people sick at your school? Is there an epidemic or something?"

"No—but—well—you see, Lucille, a lot of things have been happening lately. At school. It's pretty—uh—unusual."

"That's what I'm here for, darling! Tell me absolutely everything. Don't leave anything out."

So I told her the whole story. Everything, from the bathroom and the sound system, right on up through the macaroni and the letters on the showcase. Everything. What else could I do? Besides, I figured having a little psychic insight on the whole situation might not be a bad idea. And Eric and I were getting nowhere on our own.

When I was done, there was a long pause on the other end of the line.

"Oh, my goodness," Lucille said. "Oh my, this is serious, child. This is worse than I expected."

When I heard her say that, that cold feeling in the pit of my stomach returned, this time worse than ever. "We were just talking," I went on. "And Eric thinks that's it's not a prankster at all. He thinks the school might be haunted."

"Eric? Your friend Eric? Is he there with you?"

"Yes."

"Well, do tell him hello for me. I've always been fond of that boy. Such interesting hair. I'm pretty sure you two were friends in a previous life."

"Lucille—" I rolled my eyes at Eric, who had pretty much lost interest in watching me talk on the phone. He motioned to me that he was going upstairs. From the way he started air typing, I figured I would find him at the computer in my room.

"So what do you think, Lucille? Do you think the school might be haunted?"

Lucille made a little snorting sound. "Well, of course it's haunted. As hauntings go, I would say this case is classic! It has all the signs."

"But how can it be?" I asked. "Doesn't a place have to have a, well, a sort of a history, to be haunted? The school is brand-new!"

Lucille gasped. "You mean you don't know? Your father didn't tell you?"

"Tell me what?"

"Randy, just because someone puts up a new building doesn't mean that the spirits who haunted the place before it was built just go away."

"They don't?"

"Of course not. All ghosts who walk the earth walk it for a reason. They are tied to a particular place. It can be a place where they were very happy during their lives, or a place where they were very sad. It can be a place where they lived, or a place where they died. Or, as in the case of your school, ghosts can haunt the place where they were buried."

"Excuse me?" My heart, which had started thumping loudly when she began to tell me about ghosts, suddenly skipped a couple of beats.

"More than a hundred years ago, in the exact same spot where your school stands now, was the old Pauper's Cemetery. You know what a pauper is?"

"Sure, it's a poor person."

"That's right. Anyway, Pauper's Cemetery was where the town buried all those who were too poor for a private funeral. And it wasn't just poor people, either. Criminals were buried in pauper's graves, too, most of them. I'm surprised you didn't know, Randy. Your father and the Board of Education had a terrible time with the Historical Society when they chose that spot."

I chewed my lip, thinking hard. "I guess I remember something like that. I just didn't know what it was all about."

"Well, you do now," Lucille said. "The question is, what are you going to do about it?"

"Me?" My voice squeaked a little. I couldn't help it. "What can *I* do?"

"I wish I knew, but I don't. But the spirits are

obviously trying hard to communicate with you. They know you're psychic, even if you don't."

"Yeah—" I said uncertainly.

"And you can't go to that detention on Halloween, that's for sure." Lucille made a worried little sound on the other end of the phone.

"Why?" I had to ask. I didn't really want to know, but I still had to ask.

"Halloween is the one night in the year when the line between the dead and the living is weakest. The spirits are at their most powerful. Given everything you've told me, these entities you're dealing with are already pretty stirred up. If that detention takes place, well, all I can say is— you'll all be a bunch of sitting ducks. There will be some terrible mischief. You must try to stop them, Randy. Before Halloween."

"Hey, wait a minute. Why me?"

"Because you know, Randy. You know the truth. They always try to contact people who are sensitive to them. It's easier. So you must try to help them. You understand? You have the power, but it won't do any good if you don't use it."

"I don't want to use it! I don't care! I just want things to be normal!"

Lucille sighed again at the other end of the

line. I knew I was acting like a wimp about the whole thing, and I felt bad. But I also felt scared—really scared.

She waited a minute before answering. "If you don't try to free these spirits, something terrible is going to happen on Halloween. Something far worse than anything that has happened so far. You know it, and so do I."

When she said that, I had to bite my lip hard to keep from getting all choked up. Seriously— that's how frightened I was. "But, Lucille," I stammered. "What am I supposed to do? I don't know what to do!" I for sure sounded like a wimp now, but I didn't care.

"Randy, I can't tell you what to do because I don't know. Honestly I don't. I want to help, but I can't tell you what I don't know, can I?"

"No," I agreed. "I guess not."

"All I know is this—a ghost always haunts a place for a reason. Think about it—you and Eric. Put your heads together. I can sense he's there to help you. The spirits will try to communicate through you, but you must be open to them. Think about it—what reason would these ghosts have to haunt the school?"

I never got the chance to answer, because just then the phone went dead. Completely.

10

I raced upstairs as fast as I could go. I burst in the door of my bedroom with my heart pounding. Eric was stretched out over my bed, one arm thrown across his eyes. For a second, he looked dead. But he was only asleep—sound asleep. Over in the corner, the computer screen scrolled to a stop at the end of a screen full of text, just as the printer kicked in.

"Eric!" I shook him by the shoulder, hard. "Eric, wake up! You gotta hear this, man!"

Eric stared up at me sleepily. "That was weird, man," he mumbled. "One minute I'm at the computer, trying to decode that message, and the next, I had to lie down. I couldn't keep my eyes open."

"Are you okay? Are you sick or something?"

Eric shook his head. "Nah," he insisted. "I'm fine. It's just that it was weird."

I sat back and looked at him. "That's nothing.

Wait till you hear this. I know why the school is haunted, man. It was built on top of a cemetery."

Eric paused in mid-yawn. "No lie?"

"No lie. Lucille told me. She says it used to be a cemetery where they buried criminals and poor people and murderers and stuff. We need to figure out what the ghosts want or we're gonna be in deep trouble on Halloween! She says if we don't find a way to contact them, something horrible's going to happen at that detention! And then the phone went dead."

"Dead?" Eric's eyebrows shot up. He leapt off the bed and headed over to the computer. The screen cursor blinked patiently after the single word on the screen: Next?

Eric tore off a sheet of printout and frowned. "How could it have gone dead?" he asked me. "I was using your outside modem line and everything was working fine."

"Using it for what?"

He looked at me like I was totally dense. "To surf the InterNet, of course. There's this bulletin board there where all the members do is decode each other's messages. You know, they're like ex-spies and stuff. They come up with new codes and try to crack them all the time. It's awesome."

I still didn't get it. "So?"

Eric gathered up the sheets of printout and laid them out on my bed in a long strip. "I kept thinking about those letters scratched into the showcase. I thought it might be some kind of code or something. So I went to the bulletin board, to see if they could come up with anything."

I was getting excited. When it comes to finding the answers on a computer, Eric can be pretty creative. "What did they tell you? What did they find? Is it a code?"

Eric shrugged. "Search me. Like I told you, I fell asleep. Whatever they found is on the printout."

We started at the top page, Eric running his finger down the lists of possibilities and me peering over his shoulder.

"Look," he said. "The first thing they tried was the word Urs. They did a search of what it might mean in some other language and came up with nothing. Then, they tried it as initials. Uriah Robert Simpson, Ursula Regina Samuels. Like that."

"What good does that do?" I demanded very impatiently.

"They're just eliminating the possibilities,

okay? That's what the computer is for. To try all the combinations and eliminate the possibilities. Keep your shirt on."

He thumbed through sheet after sheet, then all at once he stopped, the color draining from his face. "Oh wow—" he said softly.

"What? What?"

He stared at me. "You said the phone went dead?"

"Yeah," I told him. "Right in the middle of my conversation. When we were talking about the ghosts. She said we had to find what it was the ghosts wanted before the haunting would stop. And then the phone went dead."

Eric stared hard at the printout. "That must've been when this happened," he said slowly. "Look. The computer was right in the middle of the initials thing when this happened. Right about the same time I fell asleep."

I looked at the place where Eric pointed, feeling a chill creep slowly up my spine.

"*Call terminated*," it read. But just below that, there were about a hundred more lines of printout, all of which said the same thing.

Urs iz hours

Urs iz hours
Urs iz hours
Urs iz hours
Urs iz hours
Urs iz hours
Urs iz hours

"But—" I couldn't even finish the question. I didn't even know what exactly it was that I wanted to ask. But then, I didn't need to finish, because that's when Eric pointed to the last line the computer had printed before it had stopped.

"Yours is ours."

We stared at each other for what seemed like a long time. Then at last I found the words to speak.

"Eric," I said, "what would you want if you were a pauper?"

He blinked. "You mean if I was poor? Like that? I don't know. I guess if you didn't have anything much, then everything you had would be important."

I grinned, suddenly feeling better than I had in weeks. "That's it! It's the things in the showcase! Remember how the stuff in the showcase was dug up from the building site? It's all stuff from the cemetery. It has to be! That's why the ghosts are there—they want their stuff back!"

Eric nodded. "I get you. It's like they piled up all the gym shoes in the pool because they wanted their shoes back. And the way they wrecked the library books. It's like they've been trying to tell us all along! They want somebody to give them their stuff back."

"Exactly! And that's just what we're going to do. We're going to get those things from the case and give them back somehow. Maybe bury them in the basement. And then the hauntings will stop."

Eric leaned back against the headboard, frowning thoughtfully. "Fine with me," he said at last. "I just have one question. How are we going to get those things from that showcase? It's locked all the time."

I smiled. "Simple," I said. "We're going to have to break in."

11

On the day of the break-in, we barely made it through our classes. Everywhere you went, both kids and teachers were jumpy, ready to accuse you of all sorts of things if you so much as looked at them funny. But in spite of that, I really tried to do what Lucille had told me—to keep myself open to the ghosts, to see if I could sense their presence. And I sensed it all right.

I could tell when one of them was close, by the way the hair on my arms stood up or when I got the cold feeling in my gut. And I sensed something else too. I sensed that they were waiting. Waiting to see if Eric and I could do what we intended to do.

I met Eric at my locker just after sixth period History class. He glanced at me and kept his voice low, in case anyone was listening.

"We'll meet downstairs," he hissed. "Music practice room. You got the mallet?"

I nodded. I'd brought a soft-headed mallet from my dad's workshop. Eric was supposed to bring the glass cutter. "You?"

He slipped a hand inside his jacket pocket and glanced around to make sure no one was looking. "Right here," he grinned. I could tell he was going to enjoy this. Like I told you, he's always been a little nuts. Stuff like danger brings out the best in him.

"Three-fifteen," he said, and jogged off down the hall.

Then at 3:30, the last school bell of the week rang and the building fell silent once again. I didn't exactly know what it was for, that bell, I'd never stayed behind that much, but I knew we had to get on with it. If we waited too long, we could get locked inside the building for the weekend. And that would have been bad. Real bad.

I closed my eyes for a minute, just to see if I could sense anything. And I did. Big time. Eric and I were supposed to be alone, there in the music room. But we weren't. The spirits were there, too. I could feel them everywhere, watching and waiting. And I couldn't help but wonder what would happen to us if we failed.

I heard a little noise as Eric got up from under the piano and stuck his head out the door to see if the coast was clear. I came out from behind a curtain, feeling my palms beginning to sweat and trying to ignore the sound of the blood pounding in my ears. One security guard was posted at the other end of the hall, just around the corner and out of sight. We could hear him, talking on his cordless phone to someone. I smiled at Eric; luck was on our side. Maybe.

In the darkened hallway the showcase seemed to give off a weird, supernatural glow—like it was expecting us, somehow. It was shining with a yellow-green light that pulsed slowly as we crept closer, hardly daring to breathe. I can't explain it, but it was there, beckoning to us in the silence of the corridor.

Eric pulled the glass cutter from his pocket, lifted it to the front of the case and bore down. With the first cut, the glass emitted a little shriek, like fingernails on a blackboard, almost as if it were in pain. I practically passed out from fright.

Eric stopped, pale and trembling. We listened. Then came the guard's voice again from down the hall. He hadn't heard it.

"Easy, man," I hissed at Eric.

He nodded wordlessly and tried again, this time muffling the sound with a corner of his coat. He worked for what seemed like hours, but the glass was thick and stubborn. His jaw was clenched and I could see there was a sheen of sweat of his forehead. Finally, he sat back and held up his hand. His wrist was shaking with the effort. I looked at the case. He'd only made a half circle.

Then we heard it—a sound coming from the opposite end of the hall. I grabbed his arm and we froze, still as statues, flattening ourselves against the wall. My hands and feet felt like blocks of ice, and beside me Eric's breath was coming fast, like panting. The sound came again, clattering metal and wheels. One of the members of the cleaning crew was coming our way. There was nothing for us to do but wait.

Then, not twenty feet away, we heard the cleaning cart turn a corner into another corridor, then go into a service elevator. The doors closed with a soft whoosh and we tried to breathe again.

Eric pressed the glass cutter against my palm and managed a shaky smile. "You try," he quietly whispered.

I knelt in front of the case and lifted the cutter, but I was so nervous it slipped from my sweaty hand and fell to the floor with a clatter. Eric just wrapped his arms across his chest and squeezed his eyes shut tight. Down the hall, the guard's voice stopped suddenly.

I leaned my head against the showcase and remembered that Lucille had said they could help you—the spirits. They could help you as well as cause trouble.

I felt the coolness of the glass against my forehead as I concentrated with all my might. Please, please, please...

It was all of I could think of. But they heard me. I know they did. In the next moment, I heard the guard's voice clearly and still coming from a safe distance away.

"Nothing," he was saying. "Just thought I heard something. Must've been the cleaning crews. Anyway, like I was telling you, about that game..."

Eric slid the cutter over to me with the toe of his shoe. I gripped it firmly in my hand. Please, I thought once more. Harder this time. And all at once, it became easy. It was like cutting butter with a hot knife. They were helping us!

I grinned goofily at Eric. I couldn't believe it! I felt the weight of the cutter in my hand, swift and sure. In another minute, a circle was completely cut into the glass.

I rose shakily to my feet, to stand watch while Eric crouched down in front of the case, wetting his lips and holding the mallet in his hand.

"Okay, ghosts," he whispered. "Here goes nothing."

Maybe we should have heard the footsteps, or maybe it was just that they were timed so perfectly with the soft taps against the showcase glass, I don't know. I only know we did it. Eric tapped out the glass clean as a whistle, and I reached in and pulled the few items that were in the case, stuffing them into our pockets as fast as I could.

Then, without looking at anything, we turned in the opposite direction toward the door to the basement, grinning at each other like a couple of fools.

And there, blocking our way, was another guard.

He was only about six feet, but he seemed like a giant. His hat was pushed far back onto his head and his gut spilled over his belt. There was a big scar running down one side of his face from his forehead to his chin. He smiled an evil smile, and dragged a nightstick from its holster and thwacked it against the palm of his hand in a way that let us know he wasn't kidding around.

"How you doin', boys? Can I see your ID?"

It's hard to explain what happened after that. Even now, when I remember it, I'm not exactly sure how it was. It's hard to pick out all the details when your whole life is flashing before your eyes. I just kept thinking that I was going to have to explain to my mom that I was expelled. I just kept thinking that now everyone was going to think Eric and I were the pranksters, the vandals responsible for everything, all of it. And it made me want to throw up. Because the more you try to say you're innocent in a situation like that, the worse it gets. We were sunk. And both of us knew it.

I snuck a look at Eric, who was blushing so hard his skin was pretty much the same color as his hair.

But we never had to show our IDs at all, because just then, the other security guard, the one who had been talking on the phone, hollered from down the hall, screaming into his telephone.

"Help! Fire! Help! FIRE! Ivy Street Middle School! Hurry!"

The guard in front of us glanced up and we all whirled around. Huge clouds of black smoke belched and billowed at the far end of the hall as the guard stood waving his arms frantically and choking from the smoke. Eric began to cough and I felt the sting of smoke in my eyes, making them water. The big guard jogged off and hollered at us over his shoulder.

"Get outside! Hurry!"

We didn't need to be told twice. We ran like heck up the stairs and out the nearest door we could find.

The weird thing is, that guard never told anyone about us. I don't know why, except that I heard he slipped on the floor in the course of trying to put out the fire and hit his head. So maybe he got amnesia. Or maybe it was the spirits who made him forget about seeing us that day. All I know is, we never got caught.

I asked Lucille about it later, and she says it was the spirits who started that fire. She says they were helping us return their possessions. It makes sense to me. Especially since they never found a fire at all, really, just this teeny little bunch of papers in a wastebasket in one of the broom closets. Some guy from the the fire department came on the six o'clock news and said they'd never seen anything like it—all that smoke from such a small blaze.

Like I say, I don't know. But it sort of feels like Lucille's right. Besides, she was right about other things. Like when she told me that ghosts don't always make your life miserable. Sometimes they can really help you out.

We never got to the basement that day either, but I don't think the spirits minded. Instead, we buried the stuff we had from the showcase in the one corner of the athletic field that was all dug up. And we figured it was all right with the ghosts, because you know something? That was the last time it was ever dug up again.

We dropped the shoe and the book and the knife, and all the other things we'd taken, into the deepest hole we could find and stamped down on the dirt, just as the fire trucks came roaring into the parking lot.

And then we just smiled at each other. It was over—you could feel it in your gut. Where I'd had the cold feeling for so long, I suddenly got a warm feeling instead, the same kind of warm glow you get when you know you've done something right.

And since that day nothing—but nothing—unusual has happened at the Ivy Street Middle School.

Oh yeah—they still cancelled Halloween that year. And we still had to go to detention, but somehow we didn't mind, Eric and me. We knew it could have been a lot worse. Besides, and this part was a little weird, too, if you ask me, about halfway through the detention, Mr. McGivern got up at the podium and told us we could all go home. Just like that. He said that we'd all been punished enough and that he knew in his heart that if there were pranksters among us, they'd learned their lesson and would never strike again.

How did he know that?

Beats me. Like I say, I'm only telling the story.

But the way I got it figured, I think maybe he's a little bit psychic, too.